DOCTOR WHO

DEATH IN THE STARS

Death in the STARS

BONNIE LANGFORD

with Jacqueline Rayner

BOOKS

1

BBC Books, an imprint of Ebury Publishing
20 Vauxhall Bridge Road
London SW1V 2SA

BBC Books is part of the Penguin Random House group of companies whose addresses
can be found at global.penguinrandomhouse.com

Doctor Who is produced in Wales by Bad Wolf with BBC Studios Productions.

Executive Producers: Russell T Davies, Julie Gardner, Jane Tranter, Joel Collins & Phil Collinson

First published by BBC Books in 2024

www.penguin.co.uk

A CIP catalogue record for this book is available from the British Library

ISBN 9781785948794

Editorial director: Albert DePetrillo
Project editor: Steve Cole
Cover design: Two Associates
Typeset by Rocket Editorial Ltd

Printed and bound in Great Britain by Clays Ltd, Elcograf S.p.A.

The authorised representative in the EEA is Penguin Random House Ireland,
Morrison Chambers, 32 Nassau Street, Dublin D02 YH68

Penguin Random House is committed to a sustainable future
for our business, our readers and our planet. This book is made
from Forest Stewardship Council® certified paper.

Contents

A dedication for the dedicated …

Thank you to all the fans of every generation who have watched an adventurer travelling through time and space in a box — sharing those stories on a box that make us think outside the box

Chapter One

Partners in Crime

'Zephonium, zeus plugs, zodiac spork ... and a carrot.' Melanie Jane Bush put the carrot in her pocket and out of her mind and crossed off the last item on her electro-clipboard. It had taken several months, but she had finally completed the inventory of the *Nosferatu II*. She loved having a project in hand, and each time she ticked off a step along the way it released as many endorphins as completing an aerobics workout. As she went off to find lunch, she was smiling a *very* satisfied smile.

Sabalom Glitz was also smiling when Mel joined him in the ship's ice-cream parlour, a beatific, beaming smile of such bliss that she knew he was hiding something. It was probably only that he had hastily substituted the smoothie he was now sipping for a double-chocolate super-sundae – but with Glitz you never quite knew. He was so cheerfully amoral that he could be planning a planet-selling scam or a multi-galaxy jewel heist and he'd have that exact same look of angelic innocence on his face.

Mel knew she wouldn't change him, not at the deepest, fundamental level at least. She wasn't even going to try. But she remained hopeful – no, more than that – she was *convinced* that she could channel his criminal tendencies towards something more worthwhile. She herself was quite painfully law-abiding; that was as much an immutable part of her as her flaming red hair. But she'd realised during her time with time-travelling righter-of-wrongs the Doctor that sometimes rules had to be disobeyed in order for good to be done.

Mel's moral compass would always point in the right direction, and Glitz would help her trample over any metaphorical Keep off the Grass signs in order to follow it. Together, they were going to be – eventually – unstoppable.

'Get you anything, Mel? Cottage cheese? Shimaleaf salad? A carrot or two?'

'I rather fancied a double-chocolate super-sundae,' she said, matching Glitz's own angelic smile. 'I deserve a treat for finishing the inventory and I think there's one left in the freezer…' She laughed as his grin gave way to awkwardness and added, 'Only joking!'

Mel went behind the counter and started to cut up some fruit, as Glitz produced the half-eaten (and now half-melted) ice-cream dish from under the table and recommenced his lunch.

Glitz had lost his previous ship, the *Nosferatu* (taken by one of Glitz's creditors, then blown to smithereens) and his previous ship's crew (sold to the same creditor for seventeen crowns each, after a failed mutiny). Luckily it had turned out that the shopping centre owned by Kane, the creditor in question, was really a starflight photon-driven spaceship and, following Kane's demise, Glitz appropriated it as his own. With a new ship (rechristened the *Nosferatu II*) and a new crew (Mel), it was soon back to business as usual for Glitz – more or less.

Keeping what had been Iceworld's ice-cream parlour in place wasn't something Glitz and Mel had discussed, but it was soon clear that neither of them had any great desire to change it. Not for sentimental reasons – Mel was too practical and Glitz too self-centred for that – but just because they both found it a handy meeting place. Now it was the heart of the ship: a combination of canteen, rec room and lounge, and they shared a meal or two there most days. It had taken time, but they'd fallen into a rhythm of cohabitation, becoming used to each other's ways and …

Mel suddenly realised that in their earliest days eating together on the *Nosferatu II*, Glitz hadn't thought twice about tucking into a triple-decker kronkburger in front of her, followed by a fudgsicle or three, all washed down with a bananaberry milkshake with extra whipped cream. But now here he was acting all coy over a mere ice-cream sundae! Was he feeling guilty for the way he generally mistreated his body? She might not be trying to change Glitz (*too* much), but if he wanted to change *himself* – well, that was certainly gratifying.

The Doctor called it 'the Mary Poppins Effect': being in the presence of someone practically perfect in every way made people want to pull their own socks up. Not that Mel considered herself practically perfect, or anywhere near it, but she did always try to set a good example…

She carried her bowl over to Glitz's table and sat down opposite him, pushing the clipboard across the pink plastic tablecloth. 'Now we know exactly what we're carrying, the next step is to work out supply and demand. Not just for the cargo, but for fixtures and fittings too. Here on page one I've listed all the temperature-regulating equipment from Iceworld that's not being used any more; that should be an easy sale to start us off. We need to look for cold-dependent species like the Ice Warriors, or perhaps planets that are experiencing rapid temperature increases. I'd say that's a fairly high priority as neither of us is qualified to carry out long-term maintenance of these systems so they'll start depreciating in value soon. Then there's—'

'Mel, Mel!' Glitz's eyebrows had risen high. '"Long-term maintenance"? "Depreciation"? You've got a lot to learn about this game. Things need to look all right and hold together long enough for a demonstration. Wasting time, effort and money on anything more than that is a mug's game.'

'And what happens when an Ice Warrior discovers he's been swindled?'

'Who knows?' Glitz waved a careless hand. 'Who cares? We'll be light years away by then!'

Mel pulled out her galactic gazetteer. 'So ... how many of these places do we have to avoid because you've done dodgy deals there before?'

Glitz cast an eye over its pages, and indicated a planet. Then another. Then four more. Then, in quick succession, another seventeen. It soon became quite tricky to find a place where he had *not* been added to a Most Wanted list.

Mel sighed. She'd known she would have her work cut out for her, but ...

'Have you ever,' she said, 'come across the idea of "repeat custom"?'

Glitz looked blank.

'You know – giving excellent service, having quality goods, so people will want to deal with you again?'

Still nothing.

Spooning up some fruit, she struggled for a way to make it clearer. 'Imagine a planet wants to make jam.'

'Jam?'

'Yes.'

'A whole planet?'

'Yes. Now a trader arrives with a ship full of ashaberries.'

He snorted. 'This entire planet decides on the jam thing and they don't even have the basic ingredients? Recipe for disaster.'

'But an *opportunity* for an ashaberry salesman. The planet's ... er ...' The story was starting to get away from her, but she was determined to make her point. 'The planet's ... chief fruit buyer sampled some of the berries and they tasted wonderful, the best ashaberries he'd ever eaten. So he bought all the trader's berries for ten grotzits a bushel, only to find out the rest of the fruit was rotten and disgusting, and they couldn't make any jam at all, so their economy collapsed and they couldn't buy anything from anyone ever again.'

'Well, the trader's clearly the victim in all of this,' said Glitz. 'There he is, just trying to make a living, and he finds himself stuck with a load of rotten ashaberries! What else is he supposed to do?'

Mel suddenly remembered that it was a shipful of rotting fruit that had led to Glitz losing his previous ship, so he would obviously be biased in this situation. But she refused to get sidetracked. 'Now imagine it was a different trader who came along. His sample ashaberries weren't quite so huge and juicy, and the fruit buyer only paid him seven grotzits. But all the berries were good and they made excellent jam, so the people asked the trader to bring them more berries, and he was able to make a deal to sell their jam for them as well! So even though he didn't get as good a price for his ashaberries to start with, in the long run he made a lot more money!'

Glitz frowned for a moment, then his face cleared. 'Right! I see what you're getting at! We're talking the long game here. Make 'em trust you, get them completely dependent, their whole economy hinging on you providing the goods, then you can raise your prices sky high and they don't have a choice!' He laughed. 'For a minute there I thought you'd lost the plot, Mel.'

Mel sighed again. A tempting image danced through her mind of a Glitz moulded to her exact requirements, who did what she wanted him to do. Thought as she wanted him to think. Behaved in exactly the right way.

Goodness, life would be so much easier!

Even so, this project – 'Operation *Tu-Two*' as she'd christened it, based on their abbreviated nickname for the ship – had potential. *Definite* potential. And while from the outside the team of strait-laced 1980s computer programmer Melanie Bush and devious futuristic wide-boy Sabalom Glitz might seem bizarre, nonsensical, ridiculous – it most certainly had potential too, in an extremely counterintuitive way.

If it didn't work out, it certainly wouldn't be for a lack of effort on Mel's part.

She abandoned the economics lesson and returned to the inventory. 'Putting aside for a moment the strange disappearance of two crates of Aldebaran whiskey—'

'There were only ever three crates!'

Mel raised her eyebrows. 'Eidetic memory, remember? But as I said – putting that aside, I'd like you to have a look at the items in storage bay eight. They seem old enough to be of Proamonian origin—'

Glitz cut across her again. 'So they might have antique value? Good thought!'

'My actual thought,' said Mel, 'was that there might be something in there to get the comms and the automatic drift control working properly again.'

Because the ship, originally from Proamon, had been masquerading as a shopping system for over 3,000 years, some of its functions – generally those relating to traversing the stars rather than keeping vegginuggets at the optimum temperature – were not operating at peak efficiency. So far this hadn't been a huge problem. While Glitz busily explored the labyrinthine depths of the moon-sized *Nosferatu II* and Mel catalogued its contents, the ship had nothing much to do except gently drift through space, and it managed that perfectly.

Unfortunately, its energy consumption was phenomenal, its communications systems more than temperamental, and it had great difficulty in maintaining a stationary orbit on the few occasions they'd stopped off at a planet for supplies.

If the ship was to be both their transport and their home in the long term, these issues had to be addressed. But the planet Proamon had been destroyed 2,000 years earlier when its sun went supernova, meaning their chances of finding any spare parts, or an engineer familiar with the ship's systems, were pretty much non-existent.

Mel finished her fruit and Glitz finished his sundae, then Glitz said he had business in what had been the shopping centre's loading bay and Mel said that he actually had business in storage bay eight with her, and Glitz eventually realised that that was, in fact, what he'd meant in the first place. So the two of them headed to the storage bays. Glitz's explorations had more or less proved there were no lost shoppers or accidentally transported wildlife in the maze of passages below decks, although Mel still kept a wary eye out just in case.

But nothing troubled them, and soon Glitz was rummaging through the shelves of components and tools that Mel had isolated from the accoutrements of Iceworld. He was unenthusiastic – nothing, he claimed, was worth even an eighth of a crown – but eventually pulled together a few bits that he thought might fit the ship's system, and shortly afterwards realised that his plan for the afternoon had always been to attempt repairs.

Several hours later, Mel felt a rush of anticipatory excitement. Although she'd been disappointed that nothing they'd found would fix the drift control, things looked a lot more promising regarding the communications systems. In her spare time, she had written a program to repair and update the communications software, but without patching up the hardware it had been pointless. Now, if Glitz's repairs had been successful ...

She slipped the floppy disk into its slot, listening to it click into place and the computer's increasing hum as it began to load. Figures on the screen showed its progress. The hum rose even more, oscillating between an ear-splitting screech and a teeth-rattling drone.

'Just think,' she said to Glitz. 'No more worries that we'll be fired upon by patrol ships if we don't respond to "State your name and origins". No more spacewalks to manually fill in landing forms at planetary docks. Now we can address the universe from the comfort of our own cabin!'

The figures on the screen were replaced by blocky green letters that read REPAIRS COMPLETE. With a click, the floppy was ejected from the disk drive. And from the speakers came the noise: *Tling, tling, tling …*

'Aha!' said Glitz. 'Opportunity knocks!'

'What do you mean?' asked Mel.

'We can, of course, now receive incoming signals too.' Glitz grinned widely. If he'd been a cartoon character, grotzit signs would have popped up in his eyes. 'That, Melanie, is the sound of money in the bank.'

Mel was almost jumping up and down with excitement as they headed for the supply station. Their first sale! They were about to make their actual very first sale!

Operation *Tu-Two* was go!

She hadn't come across supply stations like this before, but Glitz had explained how they worked.

It was a very simple concept. Platforms had been constructed in lesser-used space routes as meeting places for trading ships and travel ships. A trading ship arriving at such a platform was able to send out a signal: I'm here with supplies to sell! A travel ship arriving there could send out its own signal: I'm here to purchase supplies! Then anyone in the vicinity, buyers or sellers, could head to the station to trade.

'A captive market!' Glitz had said. 'The very best kind!'

The *Nosferatu II* had been almost on top of the station when they detected its signal, so they hoped they might be the first ship to respond. But of course they had no idea how long ago the signal had been activated, and when Mel peeped out of their viewport she saw that several spacecraft were already parked up by the platform.

'Don't you worry, my girl,' said Glitz when Mel pointed them out. 'I can outsell anyone. Put me in a room with a Dufrendon star slug and a saleslug from Slugs-R-Us Special Slug Supplies, and five minutes later the customer's slithering off with a pair of wellington boots and a galaxy-sized tub of salt and the other guy leaves empty-handed.'

Mel almost commented on the 'empty-handedness' of a slug, but that observation was probably as pointless as the one about selling ashaberries. Instead she clasped her electro-clipboard to her (even though her elephantine memory meant she could recite every item in their inventory on demand, no reminder needed), as Glitz manoeuvred the *Tu-Two* into position next to a large ship that had the name *Kazemi* on its hull. There was a refuelling stage attached to the platform, but that was occupied by a large, rather decrepit old ship – perhaps the customer they'd come to trade with? – so there was no choice other than to stay in stationary orbit nearby.

'I wish I'd had more time to work out a full pricing structure,' she told Glitz while they waited for the air-seals around the platform's access tube to solidify. 'We really should discuss our strategy before we go in …'

Glitz once again looked at her with pity in his eyes. 'Prices are based on how much money the customer has access to, not how much the goods are worth! And our strategy is persuading them that their lives will be infinitely better with our goods in their hands, rather than with money in their pockets. *Capisce?*'

'We are a legitimate trading company now, though,' Mel pointed out.

'As I always have been!' said Glitz, affronted. 'You make it sound like I've spent my life going around diddling people left, right and centre!'

Mel just shook her head and launched herself down the access chute.

How could she have gone home? How could she ever have gone home?

Pease Pottage village. Not too small, not too big. Not too near to or far from the big city, not too near to or far from the seaside. Motorway services, school, church. Florist and café, pub and newsagent.

How could you go back to the everyday 9 to 5 on a world where your biggest challenge was a late library book after Vervoids and Nestene and Bannermen?

Where you kept fit with the Emerald Exerciser on breakfast television rather than getting your adrenalin high running away from monsters?

Where you saw the same places, the same people, day after day after day …

She'd loved her time with the Doctor. But he didn't need her – at least, not after he'd regenerated into that droll-faced man whose brain calculated faster and deeper than any computer the universe had ever known.

Mel liked sorting out problems. She liked helping people. She liked organising things, getting them into shape. It was both impossible and unnecessary for the Doctor's latest incarnation to be a Melanie Bush project. He seemingly stumbled into crazy situations that no amount of planning could prepare for – or was he really thinking fifty moves ahead, rendering any planning on her part redundant? He bounced around the galaxies entirely at random – except it might well turn out he had some profound, world-shattering purpose that Mel discovered (if she was lucky) way down the line.

If you love someone, set them free ... They just weren't right for each other any more, and Mel had never been one to wear out her welcome – but she would always care deeply about that wonderful man, both the profound fool with his question-mark umbrella and the bombastic, benevolent man she'd teased about carrot juice ...

And she suddenly realised the real reason Glitz had pretended to be drinking a smoothie when she surprised him earlier. He wasn't ashamed of eating an ice-cream sundae, and he certainly wasn't concerned about his health – the missing crates of Aldebaran whiskey testified to that – but he knew that healthy eating was important to her. It had been a joke! Not a nasty joke, but a companionable one;

the equivalent of 'Oh no, did I forget your birthday? Ha, here's the present I had wrapped up all along!'

He had been teasing her. And it was the same with the carrots that she'd been finding in increasingly weird places all over the ship ever since she'd espoused their benefits (and those of their juice, of course) to him. It wasn't hazing or an attempt to drive her to distraction, just a harmless prank – and, now she came to think about it, actually quite a funny one at that.

Somehow they'd slipped from slightly awkward shipmates to partners who might not fully understand each other but were comfortable together. (He'd probably still sell her to the highest bidder if the price was right, or volunteer her for the firing squad if it was a choice between them, but she'd been aware of that from the beginning.)

How could she have gone home ...?

Mel's pre-Doctor life on Earth had been happy, because Mel was a happy person. She was the embodiment of 'make the best of it' and 'count your blessings'. If she'd gone back to Earth she would have been – yes – happy. But there was a reason she'd jumped wholeheartedly into life with the Doctor, and that was because new experiences filled her with joy. New places filled her with joy. New challenges filled her with joy.

And Glitz was, in his own way, the same. The platform ahead had looked gloomy, cold and spartan, but in her eyes, it sparkled with opportunity, and she knew he saw that sparkle too.

She had made the right decision after all, bizarre as it might have seemed to onlookers at the time. This was going to work out! This was actually going to work out!

Excitement bubbled through her as she slid down the chute.

Chapter Two

The Professionals

M el landed catlike on her feet at the bottom of the chute. Glitz was not so graceful, emitting a loud 'oof' as he thudded onto the dull concrete floor of a small, stark anteroom. Its plainness might once have been clinical and functional; now it was giving out abandoned-tower-block vibes. Memories of her deadly visit to Paradise Towers – a place that had proved the antithesis of its name – came to mind, and Mel felt her excitement start to wane.

But she put on her game face. There might be a slight musty odour in the air, but beneath that was surely the smell of success. It was time to introduce the universe to Operation *Tu-Two*. Moments from now she'd be giving their first ever sales pitch!

Deep breath. Another deep breath. Excitement was building again.

Mel pushed open the door ...

And the remaining dregs of her excitement dribbled out through the toes of her grey suede pixie boots.

The trading floor was as gloomy and grim as the antechamber. It was large and decorated with concrete pillars – perhaps intended to give the impression of a Roman forum. Some tables and chairs were scattered around the edge of the room. There were signs of technology, proving that this was not, in fact, the ancient world – a few computer screens and assorted bits of gear and gadgetry. What there was a complete absence of, was people.

Glitz was unconcerned when she pointed this out. 'Who's going to hang around here for days on the off-chance another ship happens by? They'll be sitting nice and cosy in their own ships. Let me show you how this set-up works.'

He led her around the perimeter of the room, past a row of tables to a computer terminal. Its controls were simple and intuitive, clearly designed for a place that might get traffic from all corners of the universe.

Mel was considered a computer mega-wizard back on the Earth of the twentieth century, and her instincts and intuition – not to mention that genius-level intelligence and the incredible memory – meant she could, with trial and error, find her way through most systems. She actually enjoyed the challenge, pitting her mind against a machine – as long as there wasn't a life and death struggle going on at the time. But it was quite nice for once not to have to put her brain in gear or worry about messing up.

She input details – the name of their ship; whether they were there to trade, to buy, or both; the categories of goods they offered or desired, and their chosen currency. Would-be buyers were urged to deposit funds with the platform at this point in the proceedings. This, Glitz explained, was to take advantage of the checks and balances that had been put in place to circumvent scammers, pirates and privateers. He sounded extremely put out that such a thing had been thought necessary. Mel, whose piratical experience extended no further than a school production of *The Pirates of Penzance*, thought it an extremely sensible precaution.

Once the electronic forms had been filled in, Mel pressed a button that would transmit the information to anyone else connected to the system. A slot opened at the base of the machine and two headsets were disgorged. Glitz picked them up, passing one to Mel and putting one on himself. He already looked part dandy highwayman and part dodgy bloke you met down the pub, and now he added part World War I 'Hello Girl' into the mix. Mel struggled not to giggle.

'What are these for?' she asked.

'These, my girl, are for the benefit of anyone who doesn't have a handy time machine translating for them as they traverse the ten galaxies.'

'Universal translators?' Mel said as she arranged the headphones over her ears.

'Got it in one,' said Glitz, as a soft female voice simultaneously whispered into her ear, *'Obtained via a singular unit.'*

'I don't need everything translated!' she announced to the air. 'We speak the same language! Well, sort of.'

Glitz tapped a control on the side of the device. 'It can be switched off,' he said.

Mel tapped on the same control and cut off the voice just as it finished saying, *'Device decommissioning is possible.'*

There was a vending machine near the computer terminal, although its contents weren't particularly enticing. The logo on it read in cheery letters 'GALACTASNAX' but it didn't carry anything usually considered a snack – either a healthy or unhealthy one – just ration bars and hydration pellets in blue and silver packaging.

'In case there's a long wait,' Glitz said. 'Very considerate, the folk who set this place up. If your ship's on its last legs, you can sustain life here on the platform for a while. Iron rations, water – there're probably a few bunk rooms out the back, that's the standard design.' He stepped past the vending machine, then stopped, frowned and picked up something from the floor. 'Of course, that consideration does usually come at a price.' He displayed his find – a large bronze-coloured coin.

'Someone dropped that, I suppose,' said Mel.

'That would be the logical assumption,' said Glitz. 'Careless of them. But one's man's carelessness is another man's gift from Providence.' He pointed towards a nearby table. 'Why don't you set up our stall there. I'll wander about for a bit. Just in case Providence has gifted anything else.'

Mel shot him a look.

His face groped for wide-eyed innocence. 'So I can return it to its rightful owner, of course!'

Mel sat down at the table, watching as Glitz made a circuit of the room. Every now and again he pounced on some small object on the floor, each time giving her a cheery wave as he stood up again. She waved back, amused by his antics. The chances of his finding anything worth even half a grotzit just lying around the place seemed remote – you'd have to be pretty unlucky to lose something valuable in a room as barren as this.

She brushed down her peach-coloured jumpsuit and straightened its Peter Pan collar, trying to look professional and approachable – someone might arrive any moment, and first impressions were important. She looked again at Glitz, grubbing in some dark and dusty corner. She'd need to appear especially professional and especially approachable to make up for whatever initial impression was given by her partner's ... eccentricities.

But as time passed, these precautions were proving unnecessary.

Mel found herself slumped down, elbows on the table, and she suddenly had a vision of the *Peanuts* character Lucy sitting at a little booth bearing signs saying 'PSYCHIATRIC HELP 5¢' and 'THE DOCTOR IS IN'.

A pang of regret hit.

The Doctor wasn't in, would never be in again.

What would a psychiatrist say to her on learning what she'd thrown away?

Only a handful of people had ever been given the opportunity to travel with that remarkable man. And here she was, having given all that up, stuck in a place that was half Roman forum and half multi-storey car park with a conscience-proof conman.

'What's the matter, Mel?' Glitz had finally made it back round to where she sat. 'Where's the bright-eyed and bushy-tailed young damsel I know so well?'

'Bright-eyed and bushy-tailed?' said Mel indignantly. 'I'm not Squixy the Space Squirrel!'

'Squixy the Space Squirrel?' Glitz's eyebrows rose. 'A noted nut-nibbler, I'm sure, but sadly one with which I am unfamiliar.'

'Oh, she was a puppet on a Saturday morning children's show. *Spaceship Saturday* – it was supposed to be set in the future, all gleaming white walls and flashing lights. If they'd only known what things were really like in space.' She indicated their cheerless concrete surroundings – but found herself grinning at the memories flooding her mind. 'I had a bit of a crush on the presenter. He was called Barry Day; he'd been the guitarist in Dutch Elm Disease, but he was really into space and astronomy. He'd try to teach the audience about Jupiter or comets or meteors, that sort of thing, but something would always go wrong, and he'd say –' she unconsciously slipped into a Geordie accent – '"Oh no! Squixy's gonna go …" and all the children would shout, "Nuts!". And Squixy would swoop down in her Squirrel Shuttle, and …'

She trailed off, seeing Glitz's expression. His eyebrows remained firmly aloft.

'I do remember someone telling me Earth was a civilised place before all that unfortunate Ravolox business,' he said. 'I have to conclude they were misinformed.'

Mel sighed, her happy bubble of nostalgia burst. 'I suppose you just had to be there.' She jumped to her feet, fed up with the enforced inaction. 'You mind the stall for a bit. I'm going to look for the bunk rooms.'

'This is hardly the time for grabbing forty winks.'

'Those other ships should have been alerted to our presence by the system, but no one's come down to see us,' Mel explained. 'So I thought the occupants might be somewhere else on the platform.'

She headed over to a door at the very back of the hall. It opened onto a corridor, just as gloomily concrete as everywhere else, lit by a cold grey light. She shivered, wishing she'd worn a jacket.

The corridor stretched to the left and to the right. The left-hand path ended in a single door, the right-hand path led to another junction. She went right, and then right again. Here she found more doors. The first couple opened onto rooms that were as bleak as the rest of the platform and almost as empty, containing just a few poles and slats that suggested dismantled bunks.

Mel reversed her steps and made her way to the single door at the end of the far corridor. She went through it – and gasped.

Even though she had been travelling around the universe for some time now, it was surprisingly easy to forget that she was frequently in space. The TARDIS usually went from start point to end point via the vortex and, even though the *Nosferatu II* took a more conventional route through the stars and had a small viewport, most of the time they viewed their progress on a computer monitor; it might as well have been a video game, not genuine intergalactic travel. In fact, the closest she'd ever felt to really travelling through space was an excursion on a Nostalgia Trips space-bus (which had almost ended in disaster – although that was pretty much par for the course!) back in her days with the Doctor.

Now she had stepped into space itself. A walkway, open to the stars. Oh, obviously it must have artificial gravity and some kind of oxygen bubble, but both were invisible and it felt like she could just reach out and catch a comet in her hand. She'd never experienced a darkness so rich and so black.

As her eyes grew accustomed to the darkness, she found grey amid the black. Just slashes of colour at first, then the grey itself became divided into different shades, and those shades and slashes resolved into shapes, shapes that joined together and showed her objects floating nearby.

Ships. The shapes were ships. Spaceships and more spaceships, floating nearby.

Mel started to count them, but stopped when she reached double figures; it didn't really matter what the exact number was, just that there were *a lot*. Dozens upon dozens of spaceships, not just the three or four they'd spotted on their approach, and yet not a single sign of life on the platform. And these were crowded together higgledy-piggledy, not neatly left in one of those 'outer-space parking spots', ready to receive an access chute.

This was a ship's graveyard – but who had presided over their funerals?

And how had they reached their deaths ...?

Fear swelled within her, and Mel realised her breathing had become shallow and ragged. She drew in a deep breath, calming herself – and then ran as fast as she could back to the trading hall and Glitz.

'There are ships out there!' she gasped.

'Yes, Mel, I already explained that to you. Ships come here to trade. This is a supply station.'

'Listen to me! Out there, on the dark side of the station, are hundreds of spaceships. Hundreds! So why aren't there hundreds of people in here? No –' as he started on again about people preferring to wait on their ships – 'that doesn't explain it! I think this is a trap.'

'Paranoia, Melanie! You caught that from the Doctor, always suspecting dire deeds and lurking horrors.'

'And he was usually right!' Glitz might have the cunning of a fox, but he didn't share the animal's wariness. And yet Mel knew him to have a keen sense of self-preservation. Perhaps she wasn't conveying just how sinister a sight that ship's graveyard had been.

He needed to see it for himself.

'Whoa!' called Glitz, as Mel grabbed him by the hand and dragged him to the door, but he didn't put up much resistance. By the time they reached the walkway he was following her willingly.

Her eyes adjusted immediately this time, now she knew what she was looking at. It took Glitz a moment or two more – but he did see it too.

'This is bad, very bad,' he said at last. 'Mel – I think this is a trap!'

Mel sighed. 'I did try and tell you that …'

Glitz was still staring into space. 'That's a Vinvocci freighter. A Potanuse gunship. A Wallarian wingsoarer!' Acquisitiveness took over from alarm. 'That'd be worth a fair few grotzits, even just for scrap.'

'And scrap is what we'll end up as if we don't get out of here!'

He acknowledged her then. 'Back to the *Tu-Two*?'

'Back to the *Tu-Two*. And quickly!'

In a couple of seconds they were back in the trading hall. Another second took them halfway across the floor. Half a second later they were reaching for the door that led to the anteroom where they'd first arrived.

And then it opened in front of them, and two people stepped through, hands resting on the guns strapped to their sides.

Mel was alarmed, but Glitz kept on walking. 'Casual, casual, Melanie,' he hissed out of the corner of his mouth, so she copied his nonchalance and kept walking too.

To her surprise, it worked. The two women – only slightly older than Mel in looks, but with world-weary eyes that hinted at decades of hard space-travel – gave them rough nods as they passed, and just carried on into the hall. Maybe there was no danger here after all!

She shut the door of the anteroom behind them. Even if she'd been wrong about the danger, the whole experience had been soured for her. This was not the place to launch Operation *Tu-Two*. This was not the place where their grand adventure should begin. They'd find other, better places; other, better situations. There was a whole universe out there.

Back to the *Nosferatu II* it was.

Glitz led the way into the access chute and Mel followed. She didn't exactly have the most appealing view as her partner clambered slowly upwards, grumbling the whole time about 'cheapo operations that didn't even provide a sky-lift'. At least the limited light from the phosphorescent material meant it wasn't a particularly *clear* view.

The chute wasn't rigid and bounced slightly as they climbed, a little jelly-wobble at each step taken. But soon the exit hatch of the *Nosferatu II* came in sight. Home at last.

Glitz was ahead of her, but it was Mel who spotted it first. Not that she realised initially what she was seeing. A thin black line by the hatch, the merest pencil scrawl of darkness. But it was getting longer, the pencil still writing ...

'Down!' she yelled. 'Down, down, down! Glitz! Back down *now*!'

She didn't even turn round, but let herself fall feet first, holding her face just off the floor of the chute so she could be sure Glitz was doing the same. He was. He knew her well enough by now to recognise the note of genuine fear in her voice.

The chute was breaking away from their ship!

Mel couldn't judge the distance, wasn't able to fully brace herself as she slammed through the bottom opening onto the concrete floor. Glitz was almost on top of her, then the chute rippled: a slow-motion undulation that seemed to bounce him upwards again …

She dived forward, ignoring the pain from her jarred ankles, trying to ignore the feeling that her breath was already being sucked out of her body. She stretched out her hands, one set of fingers grasping the straps of his boot, the other the heel. For a horrible moment she felt the tug of Glitz's foot trying to slip out of the boot and float free, but she found every scrap of strength inside herself and pulled him into the anteroom, slamming the cover over the chute's entrance and praying it was airtight.

It must have been, because they were soon drawing in lungfuls of wonderful, wonderful air.

But eventually, when they were no longer gaping like goldfish, Mel said, 'What do we do now? How do we get back to the ship?'

A soft, female voice inside her ear said, *'Getaway is unobtainable.'*

Chapter Three

Criminal Minds

Mel shrieked. The voice had come out of nowhere. It had been right inside her ear, but there was no one else in the room, only her and Glitz. 'Did you hear that?' she whispered.

He nodded, pointing at the headsets they were still wearing. 'Must've switched themselves on as we fell.'

He was right, of course, she'd recognised the automatic translator's voice, but that didn't explain the origin of the voice. 'What does it mean?' she whispered, on high alert now.

'Something like "Escape is impossible" would be my conjecture,' Glitz replied.

That wasn't what she meant, and her face made that clear.

Glitz tried again. 'It means a person – or persons – unknown, possibly of a hostile bent, can hear and possibly also see us. Whoever it is didn't speak loud enough to be picked up by the naked ear – but the translator has somewhat sharper senses.'

'Those two women we passed! Right, we'll see about that.'

Mel charged determinedly back towards the trading room, with Glitz trailing slightly less determinedly at her heels.

One of the women lounged at a table, studded boots stuck out in front of her; the other was thumping the side of the vending machine. Both glanced at Mel and Glitz as they entered, then looked away again, uninterested. It certainly didn't seem likely that they were responsible for the translator's words.

'Ladies, ladies!' Glitz had adopted his most charming manner, his most persuasive voice. 'What a treat it is to find such beauty in these dismal surroundings.'

Perhaps luckily for Glitz, the women's translator headsets were on the table, not on their ears.

The seated woman barked out a few syllables. 'Disclose – objective – location.'

'Why are we here?' Mel self-translated. The women just looked at each other and shrugged. Mel pointed to the headsets on the table, then the one on her head, and mimed putting it on. To her relief, they understood that.

She tried to mimic the other's style of speech in the hopes of being better understood. 'We – come – to – trade. But – danger – here. Our – ship …' She fumbled for an easy way to explain but couldn't find it, and ended up repeating herself. 'Here – is – danger.'

'Me Tarzan, you Jane,' said Glitz.

'Oh, you don't know Squixy Squirrel but you've heard of Tarzan?' said Mel, her hands firmly on her hips.

'Inability – comprehend – non-functional,' said the seated woman, looking irritated.

Mel wasn't sure how she could speak any more simply. 'Threat – here –'

Both women were scowling at her, and she felt more and more awkward. She turned to Glitz, her eyes begging him to take over. Looking exceedingly smug, he did so.

'Our objective at this location is of a mercantile nature,' he began, and the seated woman smiled and nodded. Mel blinked in astonishment as Glitz continued telling the two women everything that had happened since the *Nosferatu II* had arrived.

'It takes a while for the lingo to even out,' he murmured to Mel when he'd finished. 'If you speak simply, it makes you sound like you've swallowed a dictionary. I was betting that the opposite applied.'

Well, that had a kind of logic to it. And Mel knew that Glitz would never let her forget that he thought of it first.

'You should have some fish with your carrots, Mel,' he added. 'Brain food!'

The word 'food' seemed to be understood by the standing woman, setting off a train of thought. 'We come on vesselcraft *Marelli* due to requirement of comestibles!' she said, thumping the side of the vending machine again. 'But dispenser of nourishment is barren.'

31

To her surprise, Mel saw that the machine no longer displayed rows of nutrition bars; just a single pellet remained. It now juddered into the delivery slot and the woman snatched it up.

The mystery of the missing rations, however, was quickly solved, as Glitz pulled a handful of bars out of his pocket. 'Your observation is of the highest accuracy,' he said. 'However, by a fortunate happenstance I have on me my *personal* supply of delicious and nutritive iron rations which I am willing to let go for a *very* reasonable remittance...'

'You – Tarzan – you give sustaining comestible items to Amaryllis and Barbarian!' said the woman, indicating herself and her companion.

This confusion of names made Mel giggle, despite the aggression in the voice. Even aside from picturing Glitz as Tarzan, the idea of these two being called 'Amaryllis' and 'Barbarian' struck her as funny – the syllables from the woman's mouth certainly hadn't sounded like either name, so they were clearly an approximation from the translator. All she could say was that while 'Barbarian' wasn't too much of a reach, the stocky, pugnacious 'Amaryllis' who was now confronting them resembled a statuesque tropical flower about as much as Glitz looked like a long-haired hunk in a leopard-skin loincloth.

Glitz held the food bars just out of reach. 'As I previously articulated, I'm requesting the very reasonable price of only thirty crowns a—' Two blasters pointed straight at him. 'Ladies, ladies!' he began again.

Mel sighed. She grabbed four bars right out of Glitz's hands and passed them to Amaryllis, who grunted her thanks and passed two to the woman called – or called something vaguely like – Barbarian. They both lowered their weapons.

'We don't have time for this,' Mel said, and to her relief the women seemed to understand – perhaps the 'lingo' had started to 'even out', as Glitz had put it. 'I don't know what's happening on this station, but we need to find a way out. If we can get to your ship –' she gestured to Amaryllis and Barbarian, who were stuffing their mouths with Galactasnax – 'we can find a way back to ours later. The most important thing is to leave – all of us – now!'

Amaryllis gave a half-nod, but Barbarian looked affronted. '*Is deception device!*' came the voice of the translator. '*You no want rival trade. You want purloin space-bound ferryboat.*'

'No, honestly, that's not it at all,' Mel insisted, willing the woman to see her sincerity. 'We don't want to steal your ship – we'll even pay for passage if that would help ...'

'Mel!' came an indignant squeak from Glitz beside her, but she ignored him.

'The access chute detaching from our ship could have been an accident. Maybe these translators are faulty and what we heard was some sort of glitch, but there really are hundreds of ships out there, beyond the station, and I can't think of any good explanation for that. Come and see for yourself if you don't believe me!'

As Mel crossed the room, she spotted something out of the corner of her eye – just a hint of colour which hadn't been there a moment ago. She stopped now, her hand hovering over the door handle, and looked back.

The vending machine, which had been empty only a few moments before, was full again; Mel could see row after row of the packaged rations in their blue-and-silver wrapping with the 'GALACTASNAX!' logo. But it couldn't possibly have been refilled without her seeing it.

She was about to draw Glitz's attention to the mystery when the soft voice of the translator murmured again in her ear: '*Dynamo of hugeness has voracity.*'

'Who said that?' She spun round to see three puzzled looks. 'You heard it, though?' Three nods answered her, although all faces remained puzzled. She'd have to work out the translation herself. 'Dynamo' presumably meant some sort of machine, and 'hugeness' meant it was a big one… 'Voracity' – that signified greed or insatiable hunger. Mel was momentarily pleased that she'd been able to translate the translation so quickly, but that happiness drained away as she realised what the words implied. *Machine – big – greedy.* That meant…

'The Great Engine hungers,' said the young man who stepped through the door in front of her. 'It must be fed.'

Mel backed away as the man came further into the room. He was followed by a host of others, both men and women. All looked to be around Mel's age, the eldest no more than five or six years older, if that; the youngest perhaps in his late teens. They would have been a comical sight in their mishmash of clothes – iron gauntlets mixed with silk gowns;

spacesuits topped with woolly hats; velvet cloaks over leather aprons – but the weapons they carried, while equally jumbled, stopped anyone laughing. Blades, spikes, sticks, spears, most with a homemade appearance but clearly no less deadly for that.

Amaryllis and Barbarian raised their own weapons – and stood still in shock as the guns failed to fire.

Glitz smote his forehead and whispered to Mel, 'Of course! Weapons don't work in the trading hall. Part of that ridiculous prevention-of-piracy strategy.'

'I'm guessing that just applies to energy weapons, though,' Mel hissed back. 'Those daggers and axes will probably work just fine.'

The newcomers were spreading out, encircling them, cutting off all exits. Then they moved in. Amaryllis and Barbarian tried to fight, but they were outnumbered. Mel and Glitz, both experienced in the art of choosing their battles wisely, knew any attempt at fighting was pointless. They unhappily allowed themselves to be herded from the hall, alongside the two bruised and bleeding women.

'What is the Great Engine?' Mel asked as they were led down a corridor she'd explored before, the one with several empty rooms. 'What does it do?'

'When the Great Engine of *Seraphine* hungers no more, we will go to the promised land,' said the nearest young man.

'How nice for you,' put in Glitz. 'Dare I enquire as to what you're planning to feed to this Great Engine of yours? I happen to have a quantity of iron rat—'

Mel kicked him on the ankle and he shut up.

'You will fuel the *Seraphine* with your sacrifice,' the man said. 'When the Great Engine is full at last, we will travel to the promised land of Xuxion.'

'Xuxion? That's a planet in the Auburat system, isn't it?' said Glitz. 'Over eight light years from the nearest star casino; I'd hardly call it the promised land.'

Mel thought back to her galactic gazetteer. 'Xuxion. Capable of supporting life. Approved for colonisation, but currently uninhabited.'

'There you go. Not exactly a paradise.'

'But on the plus side, you've not been banned from it.' Despite the situation, Mel couldn't resist giving him a cheeky grin. 'Yet.'

They were at the end of the corridor now, and a door faced them. Mel had been working out their route in her head and thought she knew where it would open onto – the refuelling stage that was attached to the side of the supply station.

She was right. Through the door they went, and found themselves gazing up at a huge spaceship – not as large as the *Nosferatu II*, but certainly bigger than the average craft.

'Looks like a colony ship,' Glitz murmured. 'Built for endurance.'

And it looked as if it had endured a lot. It was battered and rusting, and the name on its side was barely legible – it was only because the young man had mentioned it that Mel was able to work out that the faded letters were supposed to say '*Seraphine*'.

A ramp was propped against the rear of the spaceship, leading to a narrow platform that hung over a circular hatch in the ship's hull. 'Fuel tank access,' hissed Glitz. Four people stood at the end of the platform, two men and two women, all young, each with head bowed. The women and one of the men wore robes – not elaborate ones; a rough T-shape with a hole cut in the top for the head. At the end of the right sleeve was a large letter E, opposite on the left sleeve was a large letter F. They each held a long piece of metal at their side as if it was a staff – perhaps further pieces of the dismantled bunks.

The fourth person was dressed all in blue, and wore a cloak and a crown as well as an ornate chain around his neck. Mel was too far away to see the regalia in any detail, but she thought they looked rather peculiar.

There was one other person, high up on the ship. Away from the ramp, on the far side of the hatch, was another platform that perched alone, and someone was sitting on it – a young woman, or perhaps a girl. Mel couldn't tell much about her, just that she was wearing a dress with some colourful pattern on it.

The leader of Mel's party stopped at the foot of the ramp, and called up to the blue-robed man. 'Finrae, we bring the stardust sacrifice!'

The man raised his head. 'Be patient. We have already hurried the rituals of preparation as there was insufficient notice of the first of the new arrivals. The Great Engine of *Seraphine* hungers, but it will not be rushed, especially now the end is near.'

Mel thought his words might answer one of the questions she'd been pondering as they were ushered through the corridors – why had she and Glitz been able to wander round the supply station for so long, to the extent that they almost left it, before being seized by these people?

Perhaps it was because they hadn't known she and Glitz were on the way until the *Nosferatu II* was almost upon them, thanks to its faulty comms. All that time she'd been sitting around in the trading hall, this man Finrae and the others had been racing through the preparations needed to sacrifice people to their ship's engine, or whatever the ridiculous rites were that they had in mind.

Mel's eyes darted all around, trying to take in as much of the surroundings as possible without making it obvious what she was doing.

It wasn't a very inspiring view.

There seemed to be just the one door to the interior of the supply station, the one they'd come through. Other than that, the only exit was from the stage directly into space, and unless they could hijack this pile of rusting junk known as the *Seraphine*, that didn't seem a realistic escape option.

She glanced at Glitz, who gave a very slight shake of the head. He'd be looking for a way out too, of course – whether a hidden door or a weak person to exploit – but clearly he hadn't found anything yet. Of course, he'd think of something soon.

Or she would.

One of them, at least.

And perhaps Glitz *had* thought of something suddenly! Subtly, very subtly, he scratched the side of his head. A casual, unimportant gesture. Except Mel noticed that he touched the side of the headset. He was switching it off.

But why? None of these people wore the translators, at least as far as she could see, and everyone here shared a common language, apart from Amaryllis and Barbarian. Mel had been tuning out the voice in her ear whenever one of these cultists – which seemed a good word to describe them – had spoken.

She realised that as the units picked up voices from some distance, talking privately was hard – but this way their words wouldn't be transmitted straight into the two women's ears. So Mel casually, oh so casually, tapped the side of her own headset, then glanced at Glitz, raising her eyebrows to invite him to speak.

'Any good at fixing teleportation devices?' he muttered.

Mel had to stop herself from shouting out, 'What?!'

Glitz's hand was in his pocket, and she caught a glimpse of a silver bangle. 'Found it in the hall earlier. Broken. Wondered why it had been left there. Guess it fell off when its owner was grabbed by our charming hosts here.'

'I might be able to fix it, but I'd need tools and parts,' Mel said.

'Well, if there were tools and parts I'd fix it myself!' said Glitz, slightly louder than was wise. A couple of heads turned to look at him, and he fluttered his eyelashes in the most ridiculous parody of innocence Mel had ever seen.

But these people didn't know they had a prince of deception in their midst, and took his expression at face value.

Mel didn't risk replying immediately. Something was niggling at her, something she'd seen earlier… No, something she'd *thought* earlier …

Yes! She had it! *Have all the bars been beamed away somehow?* That's what she'd thought when she looked at the vending machine earlier, and that was the key to unlock one of the many, many pieces of trivia stored in her mind.

She waited until all attention was elsewhere again, and whispered to Glitz, 'I've heard of Galactasnax before! They invented a vending machine that refills automatically – the goods are transmatted into it whenever it becomes empty! Which makes sense, just imagine the route of the poor delivery driver who'd have to refill them otherwise. Open up that machine back there and I bet you'll find everything we need to make the bracelet work!'

'Not just a pulchritudinous phizog, Melanie!' said Glitz. 'Right, you create a distraction, and I'll—'

'A distraction? How?' hissed Mel, but the only answer was a sharp intake of breath.

Two of Finrae's companions were moving down the ramp. The people all around had snapped to attention. Up on the platform, Finrae sank to his knees, arms raised to the heavens. 'The Great Engine is ready to receive the offering!' he declared.

It seemed that the moment for a distraction had passed.

Chapter Four

Bones

The cultists surged around the four incomers like a wave. Amaryllis and Barbarian were pressed back to back; Mel and Glitz, next to them, found themselves pinned together too. Mel felt like she was drowning, suffocating, couldn't breathe...

Then she was free again, the flow of cultists turning like the tide, leaving in its wake ... three people only.

Dozens of enthusiastic hands clutched at Barbarian's clothes as she was forced forwards, each cultist clearly wanting to be the one that delivered her to the two acolytes waiting at the bottom of the ramp. She looked tough, even without a gun, but could do nothing to save herself. Amaryllis tried to get to her friend, and Mel automatically moved to help her, but the sea of cultists was now between them and Barbarian. Using their bed-post staffs, the acolytes prodded the woman up the ramp towards Finrae.

Towards the hatch.

Mel couldn't bring herself to switch the translator back on and hear exactly what Barbarian was saying in her anguish. It was cowardly, she knew, but the look on Amaryllis's face just reinforced that decision. It was hard enough to hear someone beg and scream even in unknown words, when there was nothing she could do to help.

As the procession climbed the ramp, Finrae and the acolyte with him reached for a pair of chains that were attached to the hatch cover below and, with some effort, pulled it open.

The miasma from inside the hatch was so thick it was almost visible. Mel's head swam as the stench forced its way into her nostrils and down her throat; she thought for a moment she might faint. Beside her, Glitz made gagging noises. They'd both been in bad situations before; they knew what the smell was. It was the scent of death.

Mel blinked and blinked as her eyes began to water. This was a waking nightmare. She didn't want to process exactly what it all meant, but her brain insisted on figuring it out, insisted that she think about it. The hatch was essentially a fuel cap. The cult fed their prisoners to the Great Engine. An engine 'eats' fuel. So …

What was about to happen was …

What was about to happen, that she couldn't stop, was …

What was about to happen, that she couldn't stop but couldn't look away from, was …

The acolytes behind Barbarian gave a final push with their staffs, and she stumbled forward, a captive walking the plank. Over the edge she went, falling through the opening below with a shriek, a shriek that echoed from the hole and then just ...

Stopped.

There was silence, save from Amaryllis howling in horror.

Then a voice came from above. Mel forced herself to look through her painful eyes in which tears now formed too, and saw it was the man called Finrae speaking.

No, not speaking. Declaiming.

'You become stardust
and fuel our ship with your sacrifice,
so it does not hunger
and does not hurt.
When the ship is full
and hope is with you at last,
we will all meet at journey's end.'

It sounded to Mel like some kind of prayer – no, some kind of eulogy. Because much as she wanted to believe otherwise, she knew that Barbarian was no longer alive.

'*At journey's end,*' echoed voices all around Mel.

The chains were released, the hatch to the fuel tank clanged shut. Was that it? Had their ordeal ended?

'Saving us for later?' muttered Glitz.

A tiny dart of hope pierced Mel's terror. Time, that was what they needed, just enough time to come up with a plan. She knew they *would* come up with a plan. They *always* came up with a plan.

Or at least the Doctor did ...

Well, she'd wanted to stand on her own two feet. And she'd thought up plenty of plans completely unaided before – hadn't she?

An image crossed her mind of the Doctor stumbling across the *Seraphine* in years to come, defeating the bad guys, foiling their plans and then coming across some long-dead body with a few strands of long red hair ... And he might realise it was her and be sad, or perhaps he wouldn't realise and just think it brought to mind someone he once knew ...

... if he even remembered her at all.

She choked back a sob. That wouldn't happen! She would think of something, she would get them out of this mess somehow ...

But the hatchway was opened once more, and Amaryllis, terror-filled, was herded up the ramp. A pause to their ordeal, then, not an end. Mel's mind raced in desperation, but not a single idea came to mind as events played out for a second time.

As Finrae resumed his eulogising, Mel turned to the nearest cultist. 'Why are you doing this?' Her words were catching in her throat. 'Throwing people into your fuel tank isn't going to get you to Xuxion!'

'We will reach Xuxion, with stardust and hope!' the acolyte told her. 'Finrae says so.'

'And you believe him?'

The man shrugged. 'Without Finrae, we would have hungered and hurt,' he said, a strange rhythm to his words. 'There was sickness and starvation. We were surrounded by death, and he brought food into being by the strength of his devotion to *Seraphine*. Finrae is our protector and provider, the deliverer of Galactasnax.'

Mel almost choked. It was as though in the midst of a life and death situation, someone had been introduced to her as 'the saviour of snickerdoodles' or 'the champion of chimichangas'. Horrified laughter flooded through her.

'What's so funny?' Glitz demanded.

That made Mel laugh even more. She felt herself slipping into hysteria. 'I think …' she gasped, 'I think … I think you had to be there!'

'Mel!' The laughter fell away at Glitz's shout — he had seen them coming for her, a second before her shoulders were grabbed, and she was half pushed, half pulled towards the ramp.

She was going to die. How ridiculous was it that her last thoughts were going to be about a man who called himself 'the deliverer of Galactasnax'? And — oh my word, he didn't just call himself that. As she got nearer to Finrae, she realised that his strange cloak was made from sewn-together ration-bar wrappers, his crown and chain made from the same wrappers twisted together into a kind of rope. He was dressed like an advertising mascot; this man had made Galactasnax his whole identity, and …

And it all slotted into place, the bits and pieces she'd learned twisting together to form a hypothesis. *There was sickness and starvation … He brought food into being by the strength of his devotion …*

These people had been starving, had been dying... and then one day, perhaps, the vending machine had refilled automatically, and this man Finrae had claimed the credit for it! Probably every time the bars and capsules had been restocked since then he'd told them it was his doing – maybe he threatened to withhold food and drink unless they obeyed him. For a people who'd known starvation, food or the lack of it was a powerful motivator for loyalty.

She was sure she was right. But did it help her? Did it open up a way out? There had to be a way to use that information.

Could she show them that he wasn't special, that he wasn't the one who'd provided the food?

Could she challenge his authority?

She looked behind her. Glitz was straining to get away, but he was held fast. He was staring up at her, and she thought – she really did think – that he was trying to come to her rescue, he wasn't just trying to get away. Maybe that was wishful thinking.

But he'd never reach her, never even get near, so perhaps he *should* be trying to get away. That'd be better than both of them dying.

'Finrae's not what you think—' she began, but one of the acolytes hit her hard with his staff. She would never be allowed to say anything negative about their leader, but maybe, if they didn't understand what she was saying...

It was a feeble plan, it wouldn't work, she *knew* it wouldn't work, but she had to try.

She had only moments left.

The acolytes had opened the hatch and the ship's maw was ready to swallow her whole...

Mel was too far away to see Glitz's expression as she yelled out his name, but she imagined his distant eyes turning up towards her. She pulled her hand free and smacked its palm against the headset, switching on the translator. If only Glitz did the same...

'Unveil the ferriferous viands to them and preconise yourself to be their veritable overlord!' she hissed into the headset's mic.

Had he done what she needed? Had he heard what she'd said? Had the translator murmured to Glitz alone another version of her words: 'Show them the iron rations and announce that you're their true leader'?

'Kneel before me, for I am the God of Galactasnax!'

No one hit her.

The acolyte by the hatch had sunk to her knees.

Mel turned to see Glitz waving two handfuls of ration bars as the cult members bowed to him. Then he started to hurl bars into the crowd, like a pantomime dame throwing sweets to children in the audience.

Mel sprang into action, jumping past the acolytes and running down the ramp. If Glitz could just distract them for long enough...

But no, it wasn't going to work.

Already they were looking up, already cultists were surging towards her...

Glitz getting away would be better than both of them dying.

'Go! Now!' It didn't matter any more that they could understand what she was saying. She saw Glitz raise a hand to her, and then he ran.

Mel started to run too – but now she was heading upwards. It might draw them away from Glitz, and it might be her only hope.

'Get her!' Finrae yelled at his followers, but they all seemed bemused by the turn of events and didn't react quickly enough. Finrae himself, perhaps unused to doing his own dirty work, or perhaps thinking Mel had turned into a surprisingly cooperative offering who was about to jump into the hatch off her own bat, didn't stop her as she dodged past, accelerating towards the pirate's plank. Praying she wouldn't slip, and trying to blot out all thoughts of the hole gaping below her, Mel launched herself into the air.

She landed on the far platform, almost falling into the lap of the girl who sat there. She was perhaps 16, with chestnut braids so long that they trailed on the floor around her, and Mel now saw that her colourful dress was covered in the most intricate embroidery. The girl didn't seem scared of her, but there was none of the fanaticism or reverence Mel had seen in the other cultists' faces either. There was a trace of confusion, true, but she seemed more serene than anything.

'Go after him! And get her!' screeched Finrae, pointing first to Glitz then across the divide to Mel. 'The time is nearly upon us! We mustn't lose hope!' People below tried to follow Glitz, but found the door barred. Up on the ramp, Finrae's acolytes stepped towards the end of the platform – but balked at the gap. Finrae barked out another order and they loosed the chains, sending the hatchway slamming down. There was no longer an opening gaping below them so they would now be able to reach Mel and the girl on the separate platform, although it wouldn't be an easy climb.

Mel looked around desperately. 'Is there another way out?' she asked the girl. 'How did you get up here – did you climb across the hatch like they're doing?'

'I have my own path,' she said.

'Show me it,' said Mel. The girl didn't reply.

The acolytes were closing in. Mel wished she had a weapon – although she didn't like them, and the idea of holding a gun to someone's head made her uncomfortable to say the least, she might be able to bluff her way out of the situation …

Oh! Maybe she could try a bluff anyway!

Mel whipped something out of her pocket and held it at the girl's neck. 'Stop right where you are, or she gets it!' she shouted, trying to sound as confident and ruthless as she could. Then she turned to the girl. 'Now get me out of here!' she told her. 'Or I'll shoot you. With my … carrot-taser.'

Would they buy it? She was fairly certain there was no allotment or greengrocer's shop on the supply station, so there was a reasonable chance these people wouldn't be familiar with vegetables and their lack of offensive capabilities. The field that stopped energy weapons being used – presumably something similar to the 'state of temporal grace' in the TARDIS – was on the trading floor only, if Glitz was correct, so her threat should carry weight.

And yes – the acolytes had stopped! They were holding back!

'Please!' she hissed to the girl, which probably wasn't something that confident and ruthless people said as a rule. 'Please, just show me the way out!'

The girl rose solemnly to her feet, her Rapunzel-like hair still past her knees even now she was standing. 'Very well,' she said.

Mel tried to work out where they would go. The hull of the ship wasn't flat; it didn't look safe or easy to traverse. But what other choice did she have? Hopefully they wouldn't have to climb across the hull too far.

Or at all. To Mel's surprise, the girl moved her chair, revealing another hatch underneath. Of course! There would need to be an access point for crewmembers involved in refuelling the ship. She pulled it open –

– to reveal two young men standing below, with spears pointed up at them.

Mel gave a sigh, and let her carrot fall the ground. 'All right,' she said. 'I surrender.'

'Bring her here,' boomed Finrae from the other platform. 'The sacrifice will go ahead as planned.'

Then a shout – a very excited shout – came from below. 'Finrae! Finrae!'

He looked down. 'Speak, Watcher of the Arrow. You have news?'

'It is almost on "F", Finrae! The time has come! *The time has come!*'

Such a hubbub broke out all around – from the cultists on the ground, the acolytes standing with Finrae, the spear-wielding men climbing out of the hatch next to Mel. Finrae himself looked to the heavens, his face painted with sheer ecstasy. Only the girl didn't react.

Even from a distance, Mel could see the pure fanaticism in Finrae's eyes. This information had consumed him, meaning Mel herself was now barely even a blip on his radar. Maybe she could escape while he was distracted ...

Then the men grabbed her arms. 'Do you still want her, Finrae?'

He waved them aside, brushing away the question as a total irrelevancy. 'Lock her up. I must make preparations.'

As Mel was bundled through the second hatchway, along with the girl, Finrae's laughter echoed round and round, filling up her head. There was not a drop of humour or even humanity in the sound.

So here I am, thought Mel. In the belly of the beast. Inside the *Seraphine*. Although thankfully not in its fuel tank.

She was still alive, and while there was life, there was hope. As she was led through the drab corridors of the ship, she compiled a mental map of its twists and turns, noting the flickering lights, the broken screens and decrepit speakers in the walls, all the empty rooms. This ship could easily accommodate several hundred people, and she'd seen maybe thirty at most.

Had the others all starved to death?

How long had the *Seraphine* been at the supply station?

Had the ship's occupants died before or after they landed here?

Perhaps if she pieced their story together and understood Finrae and his people more, it might help her find a way out of this situation. Mel shot a sideways glance at the girl, still walking beside her. She must be a person of significance. If Mel got an opportunity to talk to her again alone …

Another dusty and dreary corridor, and another one and another. Finally they were led into a short passageway with a door at the end. The girl stopped at the door and opened it, then took two coins out of her pocket and handed them to the men. She stepped inside the room, and Mel was pushed after her. Bolts were shot into place on the other side.

'Did you – did you just *tip* your gaolers?' Mel asked incredulously. The girl didn't seem to understand. 'You gave them money!' Mel said.

'Oh, the offering? That's just so they can do the ritual for me. To get food, you know.' She frowned at Mel's confusion. 'New friends – like you – bring with them coins and credit bars, and they are divided between us. We offer them to Galactasnax so they will continue to bless Finrae with food for us all.'

Stealing from their victims to pay for vending-machine food. This place got more disquieting by the minute. But what was this girl's place in it? 'But you *are* a prisoner,' Mel said, unsure if it was a question or a statement. 'They did lock you in.'

'I'm Hope,' the girl replied, as if it explained everything.

Mel suddenly remembered Finrae shouting 'We mustn't lose hope!' Perhaps he wasn't talking about an emotion, he was talking about a person! Was that why they'd locked her up, so they wouldn't 'lose' her?

She looked around the room, searching for clues. There were piles of embroidered cushions on the floor. Tapestries and embroideries covered the walls, and fabric, silks and needles lay on a low table.

There was barely an inch of space in the whole room that was free from decoration. Most of the embroideries depicted people, but some showed the *Seraphine*, or objects such as Galactasnax ration bars. 'Did you embroider all of these?' Mel asked.

The girl nodded. 'All of them but that one.' She pointed to a small square of fabric that resembled an old-fashioned sampler. The word 'HOPE' was in the centre in intricate stitching, surrounded by beautiful decoration. The border was made up of little stars, white doves and ginger cats.

'Who made that one for you?' said Mel.

Hope just shrugged. 'Oh, I don't know. I think they just gave it to me because it has my name on.'

The more Mel looked around, the more she realised how restricted the subject matter of the needlework was. Apart from that one small embroidery, there were no animals, no trees, no sun or moon or sky, no other stars; there wasn't a single flower shape among the curlicues of decoration. There were no other spaceships, no planets.

Earlier, she'd banked on no one recognising a carrot. Now she was wondering if they knew about anything outside the supply station at all.

Hope reached out a hand to Mel's hair, and Mel stepped away from her. 'Please – I'd rather you didn't,' she said. She felt a bit awkward, as the girl probably didn't know that it wasn't OK to just touch someone else's hair – but it was something Mel hated. 'Oh, but it's so pretty!' people would always say in justification.

But that wasn't what Hope said. 'I don't usually have a chance to match the colours exactly,' she told Mel. 'I have to do the best I can from memory.' Mel realised the girl was holding up some skeins of silk, all orangey-red in colour. 'I think I usually get them quite close, though. Close enough to recognise everyone again, at least.'

'What do you mean, recognise everyone again?' Mel asked.

Hope indicated the embroideries on the wall. The hundreds and hundreds of silk-sewn figures. 'All the people that became stardust,' she said. 'All the people I will be with, until everyone meets again at journey's end.'

Chapter Five

Secrets and Lies

Mel took a deep breath and sat down on a pile of embroidered cushions, patting one beside her in invitation. After a moment's confusion, Hope took the hint and sat down too.

'So you're not a prisoner – but you are locked in,' said Mel. 'Your friends are throwing people in the ship's fuel tank, and they somehow expect that to get them to a planet called Xuxion. I'm having quite a hard time understanding what's going on. Could you explain it to me? Did you come here on the *Seraphine*? Did Finrae and the others?'

'Finrae and the others did,' Hope told her. 'But I was born here. I'm the baby of the beacon. I was born so the others could complete their journey. That's why I'm called Hope.'

'You were born here?' Mel hadn't been expecting that. Hope was much too old to be the child of any of the cultists she'd seen. 'Who are your parents?'

'My parents were Old Ones.' She used the past tense, but there was no emotion on Hope's face as she spoke of them, no indication of loss or grief. 'The *Seraphine* was going to Xuxion, with Old Ones and Young Ones on board. But the ship got hurt when it was in space and came to the beacon to heal. The Old Ones mended the ship, but there was no fuel, and the beacon had been hurt too so no one came to help. Then I was born. The Old Ones gave all the food to the Young Ones and me, and then became stardust.'

Mel shuddered. There was as little emotion in Hope's voice as there had been on her face, but Mel could imagine the story in between those words: the *Seraphine*, stranded in space, and the older members of the ship's crew doing all they could to ensure the children's survival, even at the cost of their own lives. 'But Finrae found food for you all?' she asked. 'The Galactasnax bars?'

Hope nodded. 'It was a blessed day,' she said. 'The last of the Old Ones became stardust and all would have perished, but Finrae brought forth Galactasnax to feed us all. He healed the beacon, so ships could come and bring us everything we need to get us to Xuxion.'

'Like the "sacrifices" to feed the Great Engine?'

Hope nodded.

Mel was beginning to get annoyed by the girl's artlessness. 'You couldn't just ask one of the ships to top you up with actual fuel?'

'The *Seraphine* is fuelled by stardust and hope,' Hope told her.

Mel was ready to tear her hair out, and was done with being tactful. 'That's ridiculous,' she said. '"Stardust and hope" aren't real, tangible things, and you do know the people who are thrown into the tank *die*?'

Then a horrifying thought struck her.

'Stardust and hope – you don't mean stardust and *Hope*? They're not going to throw *you* into the tank, are they?' Mel gave a half-laugh, trying to treat it as a ridiculous thought, because surely this girl wasn't serenely talking about her own murder ...

But Hope said, 'Oh yes. When the arrow points to "F", I will join the sacrifices, then the *Seraphine* will take us all to Xuxion.'

'"All"? Hope, you'll be dead!'

'Not once we get to Xuxion. Everyone will be together again there.'

'You think you'll just ... come to life again?' Mel realised that trying to bring logic into this discussion wouldn't work. If Hope was about 16, then she'd had that many years of indoctrination that couldn't be overturned by a two-minute conversation. This place didn't just resemble Paradise Towers in its concrete bleakness, it had other similarities as well. There, too, a bunch of children had formed their own society after being separated from their parents at a young age, and had a predictably warped view of the world they lived in. And in Paradise Towers, people were fed to the 'Great Architect' – although in that case, no one expected any of them to come alive again later.

She turned to another of Hope's statements. *When the arrow points to 'F'.* She thought of the acolytes' robes with their 'E' to 'F' decoration, which brought to mind the fuel gauge in the little VW Polo she'd had back in Pease Pottage.

They were waiting for the tank to be full!

And that man who'd appeared, the one Finrae called 'Watcher of the Arrow'. He was saying that the tank had almost been filled! Did that mean that it would soon be Hope's turn to be sacrificed? Mel knew it would be yet another pointless death, and what would happen to this group of – she searched for an adjective, and decided that 'misguided' was about as generous as she could go – young people when they realised they weren't going to Xuxion? Despair? Fear? Rage?

Hope was rummaging through her silks again. 'Would you say the colour of your clothing was closer to coral or apricot?' she said.

'I'd call it peach,' said Mel distractedly.

'That's not a colour!' Hope held up her box. 'These are all the colours, and that isn't one.'

'I'm sorry, Hope, but it is. It's like apricot – a colour named after a fruit.'

Hope just looked baffled.

'Apricot and peach – they're both fruit. A type of food,' Mel added.

'Food isn't that colour!' said Hope. 'Food is Burnt Umber wrapped up in Sapphire and Moonlight Metallic.' She pulled aside a tapestry to reveal a shelf piled with Galactasnax bars.

'There's all sorts of food—' Mel began. Then she jumped up, pulling the tapestry aside again. The bars weren't piled on a shelf – they were piled on a keyboard. 'You've got a computer!' she exclaimed.

'Oh, that's just my board of letters,' said Hope. She joined Mel in looking at it. 'See, you can push them down and they make a clicking sound. I used to like playing with it when I was little.'

'Does it work?' asked Mel, eagerly. If she had access to a computer… Well, she wasn't entirely sure what she'd do, but there had to be something positive. Perhaps she could access a plan and find a secret way out of the ship! Maybe she could even get a message out and let people know what was going on at the supply station.

'Yes, of course it works,' Hope replied. Mel felt a huge surge of relief – but her hopes were dashed almost immediately, as the girl demonstrated that the keys did indeed still make a clicking sound when she pushed them.

Mel had never been a person to give up easily. She hooked up the tapestry curtain so she could investigate further. The computer was set into the wall, rather than being a separate unit, which was awkward. The 'on' button did nothing – but then she could hardly expect it to be that simple. The *Seraphine* had electric lighting, so there was power to be found on the ship – some sort of self-charging battery, she suspected, because it certainly wasn't getting energy from the horrific 'fuel' tank. Her first step was to see if that power source could be accessed by the computer.

Mel's expertise lay in software rather than hardware, but that didn't mean she couldn't turn her hand to all aspects of a computer – building her own home system as a young teenager had taught her a lot.

But right now, she had no tools other than Hope's embroidery scissors and needles. Whatever had led to the *Seraphine* becoming stranded on the supply station might well have damaged its computer systems. Components may have perished over time – if Hope had been born here, she guessed the ship had been stuck on the platform for sixteen years or more.

But Mel looked up at that tiny embroidery of the word HOPE, and steeled her nerves.

She worked on.

At last, with a fizz and a hum, a small green cursor appeared in the top left corner of the monitor screen.

'It's never done that before!' Hope said and, for the first time, Mel heard something in her voice that wasn't passive acceptance (albeit sometimes tinged with a hint of surprise or annoyance that Mel knew nothing about the *Seraphine* and its ways). To see a touch of humanity coming through felt encouraging. Perhaps she could even turn Hope into an ally!

The computer might now be powered on, but access to its contents wasn't so easy. 'It needs an iris print,' Mel said with a groan. The chances that baby Hope's eye had been added to the system seemed remote – but she'd try it anyway.

'Hope – could you come and look into here, please?' she asked, showing her what to do.

The girl bent down and followed Mel's instructions. To Mel's delight, there was a sudden *ping!* 'It worked!' she said, overjoyed. 'It actually worked!'

As they watched, the cursor moved across the screen, letter by letter, spelling out words:

WELCOME, HOPE KOLAHRA. YOU HAVE ONE NEW MESSAGE. PLAY Y/N?

'What's that?' said Hope. 'What does "Kolahra" mean?'

'Well, I imagine it's your name,' said Mel. 'You know – like my name's Melanie Bush, yours is Hope Kolahra. Didn't you know that before?'

'N-no,' said Hope, a slight wobble in her voice.

Mel softened her tone. 'Would you like to hear your message?' she asked gently.

Hope didn't say anything. She seemed shell-shocked.

'I won't play it unless you want me to,' Mel said. 'But it might be important. You might find some answers in there.'

Hope remained quiet, but after a few moments nodded her head: a swift, birdlike nod.

Mel tapped some keys, and a voice came from the computer. A man's voice, a voice that tried to be strong but couldn't help being weak.

Captain Sandros Kolahra of the Seraphine
Day 463-slash-Upsilon.

My darling Hope. Leaving you is so hard. For many months we feared that it would be you leaving us. But you have been so strong, seizing hold of life and refusing to let it go. Your mother and I are – were – so proud.

I hope your life will be easier going forward than it has been so far. I have finally found a way to restore power to the supply station and reactivate its beacon, which was taken out in the same meteor storm that holed our fuel tank and started this terrible ordeal. I've been clinging on to life with every fibre of my being until I could be sure that help will come for you and the other children. That brings us to today. But this final repair is difficult, and I have so little energy left. I must acknowledge, however reluctantly, that once I have completed my task, this might be the day on which I say farewell.

I don't know what will happen to you; I wish I did. The Seraphine's fuel tank is already fixed, but I suspect that your future rescuers will abandon the ship or break it down for parts. I doubt you will be found by anyone willing to take on the Seraphine and take over our dreams of a new life on Xuxion.

I know that this message, therefore, is unlikely to ever reach you. But if by some blessed twist of fate you hear it, my darling, know that your mother and I named you Hope and you became known to everyone as the baby of the beacon, because everything you are and can be shone out into the universe from the moment you were born.

I know that in your new life, on whatever new world you call home, your light will still shine out brighter than the stars.

Travel on with stardust and hope.

Your loving father,

Sandros Kolahra

The voice stopped. The cursor spelled out: REPLAY Y/N?

Mel ignored it. She looked at Hope, who was staring blankly into the middle distance.

At last Hope said – very, very quietly – 'I don't understand.'

'The *Seraphine* landed here because it was damaged,' said Mel. 'Your father was the captain, and I think, perhaps, he was the last of the adults to die. He expected you all to be rescued … I don't know why you weren't. I'm sorry.'

'But he didn't say anything about feeding the engine,' said Hope. 'Why didn't he say anything about feeding the engine?'

'Because I don't think that's something real,' said Mel. She held out her arms to Hope, who just looked puzzled. Perhaps she'd never been hugged. Or not since the long-past day when her father died, at least.

Mel stepped away, and started to tap on the keyboard again. She found the ship's manifest, and saw that 200 people had started the journey – 170 adults and 30 children – but although Hope was the only child born on the supply station, she hadn't been the only new baby; June Terrij and Anris Ruckman had both been born on the journey. That took the *Seraphine*'s complement to 203.

As Mel went through the files, she saw the numbers dropping. The first deaths were only a few days after they arrived, from injuries sustained during the meteor storm. After this initial period of losses there was a gap of months where numbers seemed stable, but eventually they started to drop, day by day – that would be where lack of food started to kick in.

There were audio files too, including a captain's log – a phrase hard to take seriously after *Star Trek*, but which simply described what it was, the records kept by the ship's captain. Mel skimmed through them, but certain parts stood out.

'Terrij and Derwen have patched up the fuel tank. We've been testing anything we can find that could potentially be a fuel substitute – as yet, nothing has worked. The children have been trying to help, they know how important this is, but it's hard to get the younger ones to understand that not everything should be thrown in the tank, only certain, special things.'

'Fixing the supply station's generator and beacon is proving difficult, but we'll persevere. We had great hopes that ships might land here anyway, but FO William Burring suspects that the frequency of meteor storms in the vicinity will have caused many to deviate from their planned routes. If his calculations are correct, however, the storms will start to die down soon. If we hold on for long enough, help will come.'

'We had enough food to last us for the journey, plus another six months while we adapted to life on Xuxion. Adding in the small amount of iron rations we found on the station and implementing strict quotas, I estimate we can extend that to nine months.

To be clear, that would not cover the rest of the journey to Xuxion, but we hope to barter for both food and fuel with any visitors to the station. It's true that we have little left to barter with, but I have faith that no one would want the children to starve.

We would be willing to give any of our remaining possessions, our knowledge or our labour.'

'I am implementing a new rationing system that I hope will extend supplies for another month. Thank goodness our water recycling unit is self-powering. A human can live without food for a few weeks, but only a few days without water.'

'Miqa wrote some beautiful words for Prinderwen's wake:
We say farewell to Vez Prinderwen, as they become stardust.
They journey with us no more, but continue in our hearts,
Where they do not hunger, they do not hurt.
We started this journey together, fuelled by stardust and hope.
Have hope now, that their sacrifice is not in vain,
And they will join with us again at journey's end.
I fear that this will be the first of many times those words are read.'

'So many bodies. What do we do with them all? Where do we keep them?'

'We are prioritising the children in the distribution of rations. Perhaps it's illogical. Is it fair to leave them alone as their caretakers die all around them? But not one of us could bear to feed our own bellies while a child hungers.

One of the first things we did on arrival here was to switch off the ship's conscience machine in order to conserve power. But this is proof that no such machine was ever needed. There is no higher priority in anyone's mind than our children's futures.'

'Talla has gone. To the last, her only thoughts were of Hope. I promised her I would do everything in my power to care for our daughter. I will never break that promise – but holding off death is not within my power.'

'Just William and I are left now, apart from the children. Miqa described us as fuelled by stardust and hope. Hope – my little Hope – is the only thing that keeps me going. In many ways I am already dead, but I am a dead man who wakes up day after day and somehow still moves and speaks, just because of her.

I will not let death take me until the beacon is fixed and I have created hope for my little Hope.'

Hope had sunk into a pile of cushions partway through the playback, and didn't move after it had ended. Mel sat down beside her, not speaking. Eventually Hope raised a hand and traced a tear down her face. 'There's something wet here,' she said.

'You're crying,' said Mel. 'That's all it is.' She led Hope's hand away from her face and held it.

'Feeding the engine *isn't* real,' Hope whispered, 'like you said. We got it wrong. We got *everything* wrong. Why did we get it all so wrong?'

'Because you were just a group of scared children who didn't understand, didn't remember properly, didn't know what to do. Who'd heard the words of a funeral service more than a hundred times and twisted them into something they weren't meant to say.' Mel's heart was hurting. 'I don't know how long it was before ships started to arrive again, or why you killed newcomers who might have rescued you. Or even how! I suppose at first no one ever saw children as a threat, and now Finrae and the others are strong enough to tackle anyone, and have the element of surprise on their side.' She paused, shook her head. 'But Hope, don't you see now – you don't have to die. It won't get anyone to Xuxion. And your father wanted you to live. Your mother, too. Think of them. Not just as long-ago Old Ones, but as Sandros and Talla Kolahra.'

Hope stood up. She picked up the battered tin box that held her embroidery silks. Etched inside the lid – probably scratched with one of the pins or needles the box also held – were the letters 'TK'.

'I didn't know what it meant,' she said. 'It's just always been there. And ...' She moved over to the wall, took down the little square with 'HOPE' sewn on it. 'Look – in the corner.'

Mel looked. The letters 'TK' were there, too. 'Your mother's initials,' she said. 'She made this for you.'

'It's always been on the wall,' Hope said. 'Did she put it there?'

'Perhaps,' said Mel. 'You know, having a computer in your room like this, maybe this was your parents' room once

67

upon a time. It would make sense if it belonged to the captain of the ship. Go on, Hope. Live for them.'

Hope held the embroidery tight to her chest. 'I thought it was my destiny,' she said, almost silently.

Mel spoke lightly, but was really in earnest. 'I think having a destiny must be awfully boring. I like choosing what I'm going to be.' She laughed. 'Although things don't always go as planned. But that's part of the fun. Come on, Hope! You're free now! You get to choose what happens next in your life! I know it'll seem scary at first, but—'

Bang, bang.

The sound of a fist pounding on the door. The sound of a bolt being drawn back.

'Finrae says it's time!' came a voice. Mel recognised it as belonging to one of the men with spears.

Another bolt was drawn back.

'I don't want to go now,' whispered Hope. 'Please – I don't want to go.'

Chapter Six

Saving Hope

Before the next bolt could be drawn, Mel leapt into action. She grabbed some fabric and pushed it under the door, forming a wedge. 'Come on,' she said urgently. 'Anything heavy, anything at all, we need to move it over here.' She didn't hold out much hope of keeping the visitors out for long – there was little furniture, and most of it was lightweight.

'Hope?' came another voice from the corridor. 'Hope, you must come with us now. It's Finrae's orders!'

'Do you know these two?' Mel asked. 'Would they listen to reason?'

Hope shook her head. 'Hunter and Vance are two of Finrae's first officers,' she said. 'They, and Terrij and Marhenin and Lissi.'

'Five first officers?' said Mel. 'Isn't that overkill?' Although on reflection, she thought that might not have been the best word choice. 'What about if we played them the files, let them hear what your father said?'

'I … I don't know,' said Hope. 'No. They wouldn't stop to listen.' She gave a sort of strangled sob. 'If people don't do what Finrae wants, he'll stop the food coming!'

'Finrae doesn't make the food appear,' Mel told her. 'It happens automatically. But I don't suppose we could make anyone believe that.' She thought for a moment, trying to tune out the shouts and thuds from the other side of the door. 'What we need is to *force* everyone to listen to what your father said. And I think I might know how!'

She ran over to the computer, then thrust her hand into her pocket and drew out a floppy disk: the program she'd written to bring all the *Tu-Two*'s communication systems online. If there was power to all those speakers she'd seen as she was ushered through the ship's corridors – if they were still in working order – if they were on the same network as Hope's computer … It was a big ask. But Mel had never been afraid of going big!

'See if you can make up some more wedges for under the door,' Mel called over her shoulder. 'The longer we can keep them out, the better.'

Her tower of variables grew taller. If she could get the speakers online – if people listened – if they believed – if it drove them to change …

How could she overturn a lifetime's lessons in a day? Less than a day – maybe only a few minutes!

It worked for Hope, Mel told herself.

She glanced at Hope, tying the doorhandle to a nail in the wall with embroidery silks while shouting to the people outside that she wasn't going with them. The threads wouldn't hold, Mel thought, but it certainly proved that the girl wasn't a docile servant of fate any more.

'Glitz to Melanie, Glitz to Melanie, come in Melanie.'

'Glitz!' Mel let out a laugh of amazement – and shock. 'Where are you? How are you? And – how are you talking to me?' The voice was coming out of her headphones, but it wasn't the soft female voice used by the translator, it was definitely the voice of Mr Sabalom Glitz himself.

'Glitz to Melanie!' He wasn't answering her, hadn't heard her reply to him.

'What's happening?' Hope asked.

Mel waved at her to be quiet. This could be the thing that saved both their lives.

'I won't disclose my location, if you don't mind, in case any of those rather homicidal guys and dolls we met earlier are listening in,' Glitz continued. 'Unlikely, but caution is my watchword, as you know.' Mel snorted at that. 'I've had a little tinker with my translator unit and transformed it into a transmitter, locked on to the only working translator in the vicinity, which hopefully is still perched on your noggin. Repairs of the teleportation device continue apace, so glue that headset to your ears. I'll be using it as a focus.'

The relief, the incredible relief! Glitz was still alive, and he hadn't abandoned her. It was all going to be all right. They just had to hold on here a little longer.

Mel checked the status bar on the computer screen. Her program was loading very slowly on this creaky old system. Perhaps it didn't matter any more, though – if Glitz was coming for her (and she'd persuade him to take Hope with them too, of course), they could be back on the *Tu-Two* and speeding away any minute now.

No. Mel gave a sigh. She wasn't prepared to abandon Hope, and she couldn't leave Finrae's cultists in ignorance. They deserved to know the reality of their past – although what they decided to do with that knowledge was obviously beyond her control.

She moved over to the door to help hold off Hunter and Vance. 'A friend's on his way,' she told Hope. 'He'll get us out of here.'

'Out of – this room?'

'Out of this place! The room, the *Seraphine*, the supply station!'

'He's going to take us to Xuxion?'

Mel shook her head. 'Hardly. We're not going to just drop you off on an empty planet!'

'But it won't be empty,' Hope insisted. She turned away from the door, sweeping an arm around the room at the embroideries full of people. 'They'll all be there, waiting … for … me …'

Mel saw the exact moment when realisation struck. Hope froze. Her breathing stopped. Even her eyes were unmoving.

Then Hope screamed. A scream of pain and revulsion and disbelief; a child watching her entire world fall apart. It was nothing like the sorrow or stupefaction she'd shown earlier; this was raw horror. 'It's not true!' she shouted. 'It's not true, it's not true, it's not true. They're waiting for me on Xuxion!'

'Hope!' came a shout from the other side of the door. 'Hope, what's happening?' The pounding on the door got louder and heavier, and Mel threw all her efforts into keeping it closed.

But the men were more than a match for a small table, some fabric wedges and five foot one of Sussex computer programmer. The door crashed open, sending Mel flying into a pile of cushions. She scrambled up and grabbed hold of Hope's arm, trying to anchor her in the room, but Hope had become a sleepwalker and the men easily led her away. They couldn't seem to decide if Mel was an encumbrance or a captive, if she was being carried along with them by their will or hers as they all left the *Seraphine* by a lower door and ended up ascending the ramp that Mel had climbed only hours before.

The other cultists were no longer grouped at the bottom of the ramp but lined either side like a guard of honour. A couple were crying, and one even reached out to touch Hope's sleeve as she passed, as though hoping to be blessed.

At the top of the ramp stood Finrae, his arms flung wide to the sky, and beside him was the 'Watcher of the Arrow'. The hatchway, thankfully, wasn't yet open, but as they climbed, Finrae began to recite a modified version of the corrupted eulogy:

73

'They became stardust
to fuel our ship with their sacrifice,
so it does not hunger
and does not hurt.
Now the ship will be full
as Hope joins you at last,
we will all meet at journey's end.'

Hope didn't react. She remained a zombie.

Mel couldn't let this happen.

'Listen to me!' she cried. 'You've got this all wrong! Hope's father was the captain of the *Seraphine*. He and the other Old Ones gave up everything to keep you alive until you could be rescued.'

Finrae raised his voice over hers to recite the lines again, but she didn't give up.

'It's not Finrae who keeps you fed, either!' Mel shouted. 'Captain Kolahra's last act was finally fixing the supply station's power. Once that was done, the Galactasnax machine refilled itself automatically. As long as you keep putting in coins, you've got an everlasting food source!'

None of this was having any impact on the people around her.

Finrae and his acolyte pulled on the chains to raise the hatch. Mel didn't understand how none of them questioned this rite – nothing that produced that smell could be anything but utterly evil!

The Watcher of the Arrow stepped forward. 'The time has come. With the final sacrifice, the Great Engine will hunger no longer!' A cheer rose up from all around. 'Hope – it is time!'

Finrae gestured, and Hunter and Vance began to lead Hope towards the end of the ramp – the pirate's plank suspended above the foul pit. The girl was still in a stupor.

Mel broke free of her own escorts and lunged forward, grabbing Hope and refusing to let go. 'If the Great Engine needs one more sacrifice, then let it be me! You've stolen so much of Hope's life already. Don't take the rest. Let her be who her father wanted her to be – who she *should* have been!'

Finrae looked furious. 'You know nothing about us or the *Seraphine*. The Old Ones all died and left us! You don't speak for any of them.'

'I do!' Mel insisted. 'I'm telling you what Hope's father himself said. This all came from him. From the captain of the *Seraphine!*'

'How can he say anything?' screamed Finrae. 'How can he say anything when he's at the bottom of the tank?'

As Mel gaped in shock, an electronic screech sounded. She couldn't work out from where exactly – it came from both below and around her. But she knew what it meant.

'Captain Sandros Kolahra of the Seraphine, Day 463-slash-Upsilon. My darling Hope. Leaving you is so hard. For many months we've feared that it would be you leaving us. But you have been so strong, seizing hold of life and refusing to let it go. Your mother and I are – were – so proud ...'

Her program had kicked in! The *Seraphine's* systems were online again, and the one-time children of the ship were finally learning the truth about their past – a past that some wouldn't remember at all, or that had been overwritten and jumbled up over the years by misremembrances and lies.

The voice seemed to kick Hope out of her trance – while stupefying those around her. She threw off Hunter and Vance's grip and turned to Mel.

'He didn't want me to die,' she whispered. 'So I don't want to die.'

Mel, feeling such a wave of pity washing over her, held the girl in a tight, protective embrace.

Captain Kolahra's voice went on. Mel had planned to broadcast just the edited highlights, but without her there to control it, the system was autoplaying all the audio files – it moved on from Kolahra's last message to Hope to all the log entries made since landing on the platform. But maybe that was serendipitous, Mel thought, as she watched the faces of those around her. The captain's voice seemed to be having a hypnotic effect, and the discussions of minutiae were painting a picture of a real person – an Old One come to life. And it wasn't just the captain who was being brought to life. Almost every mention of a name – Derwen, Burring, Miqa, Prinderwen, others – caused a reaction from someone in the crowd.

'It's all tricks – it's all lies!' That was Finrae, of course. But even he seemed shellshocked.

He was the villain now, but back then he would have been just a child too, trying to make sense of a world full of loss and danger.

Still with an arm around Hope, Mel held out a hand to Finrae. 'I know this must be a shock,' she said. 'But it's going to be all right. We'll work out a way to get you all off here and find you a new home. It'll be hard, but you can put all this behind you. I'll do whatever I can to help ...'

Finrae just looked at her for a few moments, and then held out his hand too. Mel smiled, and took it.

And Finrae yanked her off her feet, spinning her round. 'You wanted to feed the Great Engine instead of her, and so you will!'

Mel screamed as she fell backwards, teetering on the edge of the hatch. Hope stumbled with her, and Mel found herself grabbing one of the girl's long plaits. She was terrified of pulling Hope into the hatch with her – but if she let go ...

Finrae seized her wrist, shaking it.

Mel was going to fall. Hope was going to fall.

Mel was falling ...

Hope was falling ...

Sabalom Glitz was there.

But he'd appeared on the rim of the hatch, and now he was falling too.

Mel's headset tumbled off her head, dropping into the gruesomeness below. 'Get us out of here!' she shrieked.

And suddenly she was nowhere.

Mel had teleported before, but usually under less stressful circumstances and using a fully functional device that was specifically for getting a person from A to B, not something cobbled together from a random piece of kit and something made for delivering biscuits. Even then, the experience hadn't always been a pleasant one. This time...

Her insides were tied in knots. So were her outsides. Her feet were around her ears, her elbows had swapped places with her knees, her intestines were looped around her neck. Or at least, that was what it felt like. She was inside nothing, a dark void – and yet it almost seemed to glow. The horrific stench from the *Seraphine*'s hatch still lingered in what might possibly be her nostrils but which were now where her kidneys used to be, and the smell was joined by a different odour, something like burned candyfloss.

Then it was over. Or was it? She still felt twisted into knots, and her arm... Her arm was all wrong! It was bigger – hairier – it had a *tattoo*! What had the device done to—

Oh. A surge of relief. It was Glitz's arm. And they hadn't become some horrific gestalt entity – as she became able to think straight, she managed to pull herself out of the heap they'd landed in. And realised that the trip was so tumultuous because Glitz hadn't just rescued Mel and Hope – already a heavy burden for a single teleport band – he'd brought Finrae along for the ride too. The cult leader must have still been touching Mel as Glitz spirited them away, or maybe he'd grabbed hold of Glitz... Well, exactly how he got there wasn't important. They just had to deal with the fact that he was there with them. Wherever 'there' turned out to be. At least, for now, the journey had rendered him unconscious.

DEATH IN THE STARS

'Thank you,' Mel panted, as Glitz sat up too.

'I believe that's what is called "perfect timing",' he commented.

'And I'm very grateful,' she said.

Glitz waved an 'it was nothing' hand, then spoiled the gesture by adding, 'As we're old friends, I'm happy to accept that gratitude in the form of goods, favours, or cold hard cash.'

'Are you indeed,' said Mel, and turned to check on Hope, who was also unconscious. It wasn't surprising that the two from the supply station were less resilient than the experienced space travellers. The girl seemed uninjured, at least. Reassured, Mel turned back to Glitz. 'So where are we?' she asked.

'Home!' said Glitz proudly. And then did a double take. 'Oh,' he said, the pride in his voice draining away as he took in their surroundings.

Mel sighed. 'Wherever we are – it's *not* the *Nosferatu II*.'

Chapter Seven

Without a Trace

They'd materialised on the flight deck of a spaceship, that at least was clear. Gleaming white and shining silver; mirrored surfaces and sharp angles; computer banks, instrument panels and screens; uncomfortable-looking high-backed chairs. Mel had been on a lot of spaceships, but this was the most ... *spaceshippy* of spaceships she'd ever seen. The USS *Enterprise* dialled up to eleven.

No, that wasn't quite it. It was reminding her of something specific ...

And then the memory popped up, transporting her back to her teenage years and weekend mornings spent in front of the television.

It was missing the atmospheric dry ice, the big button labelled 'galaxy gunge' and Squixy the Space Squirrel's squirrel shuttle, but that's what it had brought to mind: the set of *Spaceship Saturday*.

Mel half expected the captain's chair to swivel round and reveal its host, Barry Day, about to introduce the latest hit from Blondie or Sheena Easton. But no chairs spun round, and no special guests appeared. The flight deck was clean, clinical and empty.

'Were you aiming for the *Tu-Two*?' Mel asked Glitz.

'Yes!' said Glitz, with a clear 'this is in no way my fault' expression on his face. Mel had seen that expression many, many times before and knew that it did not, in any way, mean it was not his fault.

'What was your focus?'

'I didn't need one! I knew the coordinates!'

'Well, maybe you got them wrong!'

'I might not be the one with pachydermal powers of recall, but I know where I parked my own ship!'

'Then how come we're here,' Mel said, pointing to a porthole, 'and the *Tu-Two*'s over there?'

She walked over to the window, and Glitz followed. There was no mistaking the huge craft hanging in the blackness outside.

'I'm telling you, Mel, I set the correct coordinates!'

'Oh!' said Mel, realisation striking. 'I know what happened. The auto—'

Glitz finished the sentence for her. 'The automatic drift control.' He smote his forehead dramatically. 'That's what ripped away the access chute when we were climbing up it! It wasn't that snivelling screeve Finrae and his band of buffoons, it was the *Tu-Two* deciding to have a bit of a wander.'

'Well, I suppose it could have been a lot worse,' said Mel. 'What if we'd materialised out there in space?'

'It defaults to the nearest life-sustaining location,' Glitz said, spinning the silver band on his wrist. He huffed. 'Which means we would have ended up on the *Tu-Two* if this rusty bathtub hadn't parked so close.'

Mel laughed. 'Rusty bathtub' was just about the most inaccurate description of this stunning ship that there could possibly be! 'This must be that ship we saw when we arrived at the station,' she said. 'The *Kazemi*.'

'Reckon you can work out the coordinates to get us over there?' Glitz asked.

'Only if I can pinpoint where we are now. But if it defaults to the nearest life-sustaining location, absolute accuracy doesn't really matter.' She noticed Glitz was screwing up his nose. 'Except that was just a guess of yours, wasn't it?'

'I prefer the term "informed speculation",' he said.

Mel sighed. 'Well, the coordinates shouldn't be too hard to calculate, it's getting a reading from here that's the issue. If only there was a crew …' She spotted an intercom on the wall and pressed its button. 'Hello? This is Melanie Bush, is there anyone on board?'

They waited for a few moments. Nothing. Mel tried again. Still nothing.

'The crew probably became engine-food ages ago.' Glitz looked serious for a moment, perhaps contemplating the fragility of life – then ruined it all by grinning and saying, 'Bet there's some stuff on here that's worth a few grotzits, though!' He began to prowl around the room, examining the futuristic fixtures and fittings.

'Let me have a look at the bangle,' said Mel, holding out a hand as he passed by. 'If I can get into a computer, I should be able to write a program to determine what course correction it implemented, then reverse—'

'Careful!' barked Glitz, as she went to take the teleport device from him. 'You don't want to end up in the depths of the underworld! Press that button and you'll be zapped back down there again.'

Mel gingerly accepted the bracelet and examined it just as carefully. She might have to take it apart to access its circuitry, and that was risky. Embroidery scissors and needles wouldn't cut it this time. 'I'm going to need tools,' she told Glitz. 'I don't suppose there'll be a sonic screwdriver, but something like a Laserson probe would do ...'

'I had a sonic screwdriver once,' said Glitz. 'Good piece of kit, that. Won it off this beaky bloke in velvet togs in a game of Find the Lady.'

'Won it, or "won" it?' asked Mel.

Glitz threw up his hands. 'It was a perfectly legitimate game! It's not my fault he didn't realise we were using Sontaran playing cards.'

Mel took a moment to work that out. 'Oh, I see. A clone race – all male. There wasn't a lady to find.'

'There. *You* get it, Mel! Didn't have it for long, though. I was merrily walking along one day, minding my own business, when I trip over a scarf that someone's only gone and tied across the passageway. This tall feller, all teeth and curls, he helps me up, and next time I reach in my pocket, the sonic screwdriver's gone and there's a paper bag full of tiny gelatinous humanoids in its place! Robbed, I was! Me!'

Mel giggled. Glitz was firmly in favour of the idea of honour among thieves, but only when it applied to other people. 'See if you can find a microscope too,' she told him. 'And a clamp would be useful.'

Still masquerading as an upright citizen, Glitz looked scandalised. 'You want me to *loot* this empty ship?'

Mel decided to play into it. 'I know it goes against your entire moral code.' She gave an exaggerated sigh. 'Oh well, I suppose we'll be stuck here for good. But it's worth it to keep you on the straight and narrow.'

She grinned and Glitz grinned back at her. 'Whatever you say, boss,' he called back over his shoulder as he headed off.

There was a mumbling sigh from the floor, and Mel went and knelt beside Hope, who was beginning to stir. After a few minutes the girl was awake enough to be helped up and guided to a chair. She drew in a sharp breath when she saw the unconscious Finrae.

'He can't hurt you,' Mel told her, gently. 'It'll be all right. Everything will be all right.'

'Is this ... is this Xuxion?' asked the girl.

Mel shook her head. 'No, it's another spaceship.' She showed Hope the bangle. 'This is a teleport bracelet. If you push this button here – no!' she said sharply, as the girl reached for it, then apologised: 'I'm sorry, I didn't mean to shout at you. But pressing it would take us back to the *Seraphine* again, and that's not a good idea. I was just trying to explain how we got here. My friend Glitz has gone looking for tools now, and then we'll find a way back to our own ship – that one out there, the *Nosferatu II*.' She pointed to the porthole and the spaceship that still hung in the void. 'Don't worry, Hope. We're going to look after you. When you're ready, we'll take you anywhere you want to go.' She smiled. 'Or you'd be a welcome guest for as long as you want to stay.'

'What about ...?' Hope was looking at Finrae again.

'I don't know,' said Mel, looking too. 'But we won't let him hurt you again, that's for sure.' Hold on – had that been the tiniest flicker of an eyelid? Better to be safe than sorry. 'Let's see if we can find a rope or a cable or something – we need to tie him down before he wakes up.'

Hope rose from her seat and took a step across the flight deck, just past Finrae. 'I can see a cable—'

Mel caught sight of movement out of the corner of her eye, too late. Finrae had leapt at the girl so fast that he must have been feigning unconsciousness for at least a minute or two. Nobody could go from 0 to 60 like that just after coming round.

Hope shrieked.

Mel slowly raised her arms to show she was no threat as she turned towards the young man and the terrified girl.

Finrae had one arm crooked around Hope's neck, and beckoned to Mel with his free hand. 'Give me that wrist thing.'

He wanted the teleport bangle. Their most promising – perhaps their only – way to return to the *Tu-Two*.

Mel felt sick. Finrae was so much bigger than Hope. He could snap her neck in a heartbeat.

She handed the bracelet to him.

Finrae put it on his wrist. 'Tell me how to use it!' he demanded. 'I have to go back to the *Seraphine* – and she's coming with me.'

Glitz charged in, summoned by Hope's shout. He skittered to a halt as he saw what was happening, and there was a moment of distraction, a moment when Finrae's attention slipped, his grip loosened and Hope pulled away ...

But the moment wasn't quite long enough. Finrae grabbed hold of Hope's arm, and with the other pulled something out of his pocket and pointed it at Glitz. 'Stay back or I'll shoot!'

For a second, Mel couldn't see what he was holding, just that it was something ... orange? And then Finrae shifted slightly and it became clear that he was threatening Glitz with ... a carrot.

Her carrot.

The carrot she had claimed to be a weapon.

Glitz's eyes were almost popping out of his head, and Mel hoped he wouldn't say anything to give it away. Finrae might not be armed, but he was still dangerous. He had hold of Hope's arm, and he had the teleport bracelet. They needed to act with caution.

'Let's talk about this ...' Mel began, but Finrae glowered at her.

'If you don't tell me how to use it, I'll shoot her,' he said. 'It doesn't matter if she's dead or alive when she goes in the fuel tank. We'll get to Xuxion either way.'

'Finrae, a lot's happened today,' Mel said gently. 'It must have been as much a shock to you as to everyone else. We'll help you find a way forward from here. After all, you did what you thought was best, I'm sure. You looked after all the children from the *Seraphine*. Made sure they had food and water.'

'Yes!' said Finrae. 'They would all have died if I hadn't been chosen!'

'Chosen by the captain, do you mean? To look after the others once he'd gone?'

'No. Chosen by Galactasnax!' His voice became hushed, reverential. 'We were in the hall when the lights came on. A pure white light streamed from Galactasnax's cabinet, right onto me!'

That was when the captain restored the power, Mel thought. The vending machine switched itself on. And Finrae just happened to be standing in front of it.

'I approached the cabinet and begged Galactasnax to bless us again with sustenance, as it had done when we first arrived. The tokens of our love were stacked beside it—'

'You put in a coin,' Mel realised.

'And Galactasnax heard me! It gave me enough food for everyone! That showed everyone that I was the true leader, not Captain Kolahra. We threw him in the tank and, from that day, we had food and light and warmth – because of me!'

Mel felt sick. But there was one question she still wanted to know the answer to. 'When ships started to arrive, why did you kill the people on them? Why not let them help you? They could have found you a new home, a better home.'

'They wouldn't have let me be in charge, though, would they? Old Ones always stop you doing what you want. I was the one chosen by Galactasnax, so everyone had to do what I said. Now we're going to go to Xuxion and I'll still be in charge there, so it'll be OK.'

If only Captain Kolahra hadn't turned off the Seraphine's *conscience machine*, thought Mel. But even in that brief moment, she knew she didn't really believe that. Mel was a firm believer in free will – even if that freedom led ultimately to evil. Even if it led to this ghastly situation, where Finrae was still yelling about taking Hope back to the *Seraphine*.

As Finrae shouted, Hope's expression changed from fear to calmness.

'I'm sorry, Mel,' she said. 'I have to go with Finrae. I told you before. It's my destiny.'

Mel felt despair coursing through her. She shot a glance at Glitz. Maybe if they both charged at him from different directions, took him by surprise... But to her frustration Glitz shook his head, as Hope spoke again – this time to Finrae.

'It's all right,' she said. 'Mel showed me which button to press to go back to the *Seraphine*.' She twisted, looking into his eyes as she reached for the bangle on his wrist.

'Hope, no!' screamed Mel.

Hope slammed her hand down on the button – and wrenched her other arm from his grip. Startled, Finrae let go, and they each lost their balance, the momentum throwing them apart. Hope fell to the floor, and Finrae thumped into a panel of instruments – and then, in the splittest of split seconds, before Mel even had time to take a breath to scream again, he vanished.

A single carrot tumbled to the floor where he had been.

If Mel couldn't quite believe what had happened, that was nothing to the disbelief on Hope's face. 'Did you see what I did?' she whispered. 'Did you see what I did?'

'I thought you had something in mind, junior,' said Glitz. ' Didn't expect that, though.'

'That was brave,' said Mel. 'You might have been hurt.'

'I knew that thing couldn't hurt me. I worked it out back on the *Seraphine*.'

'Because you didn't think I'd really threaten you?'

'Because it didn't smell like a weapon. It smelled... I don't know.'

'Carroty?' Glitz suggested.

Mel thought she understood. Hope had spent her life in a metal prison with the stench of death all around, drinking recycled water and eating nothing but manufactured rations. *Eau de carotte* wasn't exactly Chanel No.5, but it spoke of freshness and growth, things Hope had never experienced before.

There was silence for a few seconds, then the girl said, 'I think I did hurt my leg, though.'

Mel hurried over to look at her leg – but somehow found herself hugging her tight instead. 'Oh Hope,' she said. 'Your father would be so proud of you.'

'That's all well and good,' said Glitz. 'But how are we going to get back to the *Tu-Two*?'

Mel had been thinking the same, but Hope's wellbeing was her priority right now. 'Oh, we'll find a way. The *Tu-Two*'s only just over there, and this ship is so advanced, it's bound to have shuttlecraft – or maybe spacesuits that'll let us spacewalk across! That could be—'

A noise exploded across her words. An electronic noise. Then more noises. Lights flickered to life on the panel that Finrae had crashed into. The screen in front of Mel also came to life. A digital voice announced: 'Emergency evasion protocols initiated.'

'What …?' began Glitz.

But Mel was looking out of the porthole. Looking at their home, their wonderful *Tu-Two*, as it receded into the distance. Too far to spacewalk. Too far for a shuttle.

'Oh no,' she said. 'We're moving!'

Chapter Eight

CSI: Crime Scene Investigation

Mel and Glitz conferred quietly in a corner, the *Nosferatu II* already little more than a distant speck in space.

'We've got two options,' said Mel. 'If there's a shuttlecraft – one with a decent range, that is – we can use that to return to the *Tu-Two*. Otherwise, our only hope is finding a way to steer the whole ship back the way we came.'

She glanced over at an open door on one side of the deck. They'd found a little one-person sleep compartment inside, and Hope was inside, lying down. Hope was the reason they were whispering. If she was asleep, they didn't want to wake her up – and if she was awake, they didn't want to risk upsetting her.

Mel couldn't forget the explosion of guilt Hope had experienced when she realised the truth about the sacrifices to the *Seraphine*; that guilt mustn't be reawakened.

If Hope thought that her actions against Finrae had doomed them all – actions that she was clearly so proud of! – Mel was worried it would destroy her.

After the adrenalin had faded, the girl had gone back to being passive, even apathetic – but at least they'd discovered that there was a different, stronger Hope inside. With time, Mel thought, Hope might be able to become that person for good. But she wouldn't have much of a future if they were stuck on an empty ship forever.

'I'll explore the computer, while you explore the ship,' Mel told Glitz. 'Look for a shuttle, of course, but food would be good too. One carrot and a couple of Galactasnax bars won't last us very long.'

Glitz groaned. 'What I wouldn't do for a double-chocolate super-sundae right about now,' he said. 'Or even half a grapefruit and a spoonful of cottage cheese! Still, I suppose we're better off than that lot back at the beacon.'

'What do you mean?' asked Mel.

'Well, Melanie, it was your idea – cannibalising that vending machine to repair the teleport bracelet. No more infinite refills of iron rations for them!'

There was a worried call of 'Mel?' from the sleep compartment, and Mel managed to change her gasp of horror into a yawn. 'Goodness, I'm tired!' she said loudly. 'I hope there are some more beds on board!'

Hope seemed satisfied by that, but Glitz rolled his eyes. 'Very convincing, Mel, very convincing. You should go on the stage! And no need to feel sorry for those juvenile miscreants. All they have to do is take the drastic step of *not* murdering everyone on the next ship that comes along and it'll all be peachy.'

'Maybe. So long as it comes along in time,' said Mel. 'I suppose there's nothing we can do about that just now.' She took a deep breath. 'Right then. You go and look for that shuttle, I'll stay here and work on the computer.' And she added, knowing that it would make no difference at all to his behaviour, 'Please be careful. Don't mess with anything. Or pocket everything that's not nailed down.'

And he answered, with both of them knowing he didn't mean it in the slightest, 'Cross my heart, Mel. Cross my precious heart!'

With Glitz gone, Mel turned with relief to the computer. Computers were so much easier to deal with than people. If a computer *did* do something unexpected, it was likely down to operator error – the computer hadn't suddenly succumbed to its emotions.

But as minute after minute went by, Mel started to succumb to frustration and impatience. The computer hadn't needed a password, or a finger- or iris-print. She'd been able to get inside easily, once it had 'woken up'. But that was as far as she could go.

Everything within was set out logically. The code structure looked consistent with many others she was familiar with. She just couldn't work it out. It wasn't a language barrier as such. It was more like a cipher. Mel had experience of ciphers, she'd even managed to reverse-engineer them before – in fact, when the Doctor had taken her to visit a friend of his at Bletchley Park, she'd had a dozen job offers before lunchtime – but she knew it was a task that could take months. And she didn't think this was a *literal* cipher – there was no point searching the ship in case someone had carelessly left a sticky note on their desk with the key. There was just a gap between her and the code that she couldn't jump. She needed to find some way to bridge that gap, and right now, she was completely out of ideas.

Time for a change of scene. She popped her head round the door of the tiny bedroom. 'I'm going to look for Glitz,' she told Hope. 'Will you be all right on your own?'

Hope sat up. 'I'd rather come with you,' she said. 'If that's all right.'

'Of course it's all right!' Mel assured her. She crooked an arm. 'You can lean on me.'

Mel had felt at home on the flight deck. Not just because it embodied televisual nostalgia, but because it was well-ordered and impersonal, an efficient working environment. But now, delving deeper into the spaceship, it was harder to ignore the fact that real people had once been here. The vibe changed from clinical emptiness to ghost town, and Mel found herself becoming quieter and more cautious the deeper they explored.

The flight deck took up the whole front section of the ship. A corridor then split the middle section. Immediately to the left was a shuttle bay with one landing craft, and space for another one. There was an airlock, and a locked cabinet beside it with dusty spacesuits visible through a transparent door. There was also a notable absence of Glitz, who had ostensibly been searching for this exact place. For a second, an unpleasant thought crossed Mel's mind... but no. Not only would they have heard a shuttle leave, she really couldn't believe he'd desert her in circumstances that didn't benefit him. Besides, the correlation between a missing shuttle and a missing crew was obvious: that second shuttle was somewhere on or near the supply station and had been gone for years.

Mel did climb inside the remaining shuttle to check it out. As soon as she entered the cockpit it scanned her, and informed her that only authorised users were permitted. Damn. Perhaps she'd find a way around that eventually, but it meant that a shuttle was definitely not an instant solution to their problem.

She refused to slip into pessimism. They were safe, they had oxygen; as long as there was food and water on board, they would be OK. The *Nosferatu II* would be waiting for them, however long it took them to find a way back to it.

Opposite the shuttle bay was access to the engine room, which was something Mel had no interest in exploring right now. 'Glitz!' she called out, just in case he was somewhere inside, but there was no answer, so they moved on to the next door, which led to a gleaming, high-tech galley. That was where they saw the first hint of any kind of activity: the automatic running of a waste disposal system (labelled the

'Vio-bot') and a droning noise that Mel suspected was the activation of a sterilisation field. That explained why there was no evidence of old or rotting food.

They found a large store cupboard full of sealed containers with labels such as 'protein', 'fibre' or 'carbohydrate' – words that Hope happily recognised from the nutritional content list on Galactasnax bar wrappers. She started coming out of her shell again as Mel tried to explain the intricacies of a non-Galactasnax diet, and how food preparation was generally more complex than just removing a wrapper. It was a difficult job. How to describe an egg to someone with no notion of chickens or birds or even life cycles? Even mention of the humble carrot needed to touch on ideas of plants, of growth, of seeds. Mel had never really considered the complexity of a loaf of bread – the production of flour, the mechanism of yeast, the essential addition of heat and time. But Hope found it all fascinating, asking questions that Mel – who knew a lot more about electronics than food science – found increasingly hard to answer.

Opposite the galley was a room set up with a large table, presumably where the crew ate, and next to that came a recreation room containing screens, books and games, including a Space Invaders arcade machine. Across the corridor there were crew quarters: two dormitories with five and three beds respectively, and a room that called itself a medical centre, with a small bunkroom attached. Counting the one off the flight deck, that was ten berths overall. Ten seemed a small crew for what had looked like a pretty large ship when they'd first sighted it – but then the huge *Nosferatu II* having a crew of only two would appear pretty strange to onlookers.

That left one door at the very end of the corridor. Presumably Glitz was behind it somewhere, as he wasn't to be found anywhere else on the ship. Mel opened it –

– and the shout of 'Hello?' died on her lips.

On the other side of the door there was a jungle.

That was her first impression, anyway. Her second was also that it was a jungle – but bizarrely, a jungle made out of... lettuce. Or something that looked very like lettuce, anyway. The chances that this was a food plant rather than an ornamental plant seemed high.

Inside there were walls and towers covered in plants: a maze of verdancy. As Mel looked closer, she realised that the walls and towers were covered with shelves of individual plants, although they were so overgrown and entwined that their origin scarcely mattered. Their roots hung down not into soil, but into a clear liquid. 'Oh!' she said, realisation striking. 'It's a hydroponic garden!' Mel had come across hydroponics before – although the Hydroponics Centre on the *Hyperion III* had been used for growing something rather more violent than lollo rossa. 'Glitz?' she called, once the surprise had died down.

A muffled shout came from deep inside. 'Mel! Over here! Bring weapons!'

'Are you in danger?'

'Just bring weapons! Now!'

Mel hurried back to Hope, who was waiting for her in the doorway. 'Stay exactly where you are,' she ordered. 'Do not go inside. I'll be back in a moment.' She ran to the galley and loaded up with anything that might pass as a weapon – knives, of course, a cleaver, even a small blow-torch.

Back at the hydroponic garden, she handed Hope a knife. 'For self-protection,' she said, adding with a confidence she didn't feel: 'But you won't need it.'

Leaving the scared girl in the doorway again, she began to push her way through the plants.

It wasn't just lettuce that blocked her way. The place was a labyrinth of overgrown vines and snarled shrubs, a garden gone wild. She had to use a knife to cut her way through. Mel felt like the prince in Sleeping Beauty – although she was most definitely not going to kiss Glitz when she finally found him.

She created a path through plants bearing all sorts of fruit, some that resembled ones she knew, like melons, cucumbers and capsicums, some heavy with berries of all colours, some that looked like nothing she'd seen before.

There were thickets of beautifully scented herbs too, that reminded her of mint, basil and lemon balm, and rows and rows of red and purple root vegetables – bulbous rather than long and thin, but they smelled like carrots. The fruits that smelled like tomatoes also looked exactly like tomatoes. Surely they *were* tomatoes!

'Glitz!' Mel hissed as she crawled under a canopy of bushes laden with rose-pink berries. 'Glitz, where are you?'

'Over here!' came his voice at full volume – he wasn't worried about alerting enemies to his position. That had to be a good sign.

Finally, with leaves in her hair and water dripping down her neck, Mel found him. Her partner was at the very back of the enclosure, a flat, featureless white wall.

'You don't seem to be in imminent danger,' she panted, showing him the array of improvised weaponry she was toting.

'Well, not imminent as such,' he said. 'But safe is indubitably better than sorry. Pass me a blade, if you would be so good.'

'Why?' asked Mel.

'So I can get through here!' Glitz gestured at the nondescript wall.

Mel came forward to see for herself what he was indicating – and there it was, the almost imperceptible crack of a door. 'Do you know what's on the other side?'

'Not the faintest. Hence the dual-purpose implements for both access and protection.'

Mel held out a knife – but didn't let go of it immediately. 'It might open onto something dangerous. We could be sucked into a turbine or flung out into space!'

'True,' said Glitz. 'Or there might be a hoard of gold, or jewels, or jethrik!'

'Better poor and safe than rich and dead.'

Glitz looked at her. 'Remind me again how we became friends, Mel?'

She chuckled and gave him the knife. 'Oh, all right, then. I've not been having much luck with the computer system, and the shuttle seems a lost cause too – we can't really overlook any chance to find something that'll help us get home.'

While Glitz tried to prise the door open, Mel moved further along the wall, but her examinations found nothing. At last, Glitz gave a cry of victory, and she returned to him in time to see a panel slide back. He gestured for Mel to go through first, but having seen through his chivalry, she refused the offer.

Grumbling something about 'ingratitude', Glitz stepped into the room beyond. Mel, amused, followed.

The space was as clean and clinical as the flight deck or the galley but, unlike them, its function wasn't obvious. It was made for a very definite purpose, that was clear – it was just that neither Mel nor Glitz could be sure what that purpose was.

A rectangular structure ran the width of the room – an opaque, shallow box on its side with ten indentations.

Mel had never seen anything like it before. It resembled a vacuum-formed container for larger-than-life-sized jelly babies – the bigger version of the gelatinous humanoids Glitz had once found in his pocket – or perhaps a mould to dip into wax to make giant human-shaped candles. The logical conclusion was that this thing, whatever it was, was made for ten people to stand in. That fitted well with Mel's assumption that the ship had a ten-person crew.

Oh! Could it be a transportation device? If it was a teleport, all their problems would be solved!

But when Mel cautiously looked inside one of the 'moulds', she couldn't see any controls. There was nothing on the walls of the room, and no way past the box to see if there was something behind it. Perhaps the crew weren't human. They might need to come here to be recharged.

But then why were there ten beds, a galley, and what was basically a giant vertical kitchen garden?

They looked all around and found nothing. Not the slightest clue. It was even more frustrating than Mel's attempts to access the flight-deck computer. At least there she could keep trying different approaches, but here they'd reached a dead end.

Admitting defeat, Mel and Glitz made their way back through the maze of greenery to Hope. 'It's all clear – nothing dangerous,' Mel told her. Then she yawned – for real, this time. 'I don't know about you two, but I need some sleep. Let's get some rest, and we can regroup later.'

Hope looked disappointed. 'Oh. I …' She stopped.

'What is it?' Mel asked.

'I … I'd like to go inside.' She drew in a deep breath, an almost beatific smile on her face. 'I've never been somewhere so wonderful. All the green … and the smells …'

Mel was going to suggest it might be better to wait until they'd all rested, but then she realised – this was the first time she'd seen Hope smile. She didn't want to take that smile away.

'Will you be all right on your own?' she asked.

Hope nodded. 'All the green things, they make me feel safe. I don't know why, but they do.'

'Then go and wander through the garden to your heart's content,' Mel said. 'And how about you pick some fruit and vegetables for later? We do need to eat, after all.'

'Good idea,' said Glitz. He pointed out a vine, heavy with blue-black fruit clusters. 'Those look like grapes; if they taste like grapes too, I guarantee they'll erase all thoughts of Galactasnax from your mind. Especially in fermented liquid form.' He muttered that last bit under his breath, before adding aloud: 'Go on, junior, try one!'

Hope looked at Mel as though for permission, and Mel was about to give it when she caught sight of Glitz's face. The slightest hint of a fox-like, watchful expression. He couldn't – he couldn't be getting Hope to *test the fruit*, could he?

Mel leapt forward and plucked a grape from its stem. 'As the man who rescued us from the *Seraphine*, the honour belongs to you, Glitz.'

She stared him in the eyes.

He stared back.

Then he shook his head in defeat, and popped the grape in his mouth.

'Good?' asked Mel.

Glitz nodded. 'A bit sharp.'

'We'll get along then,' said Mel. She picked some more grapes and shared them between herself and Hope. They had a wonderful flavour, just the right amount of tartness.

Hope laughed out loud with delight – her first laugh in Mel's presence. Maybe even her first ever laugh?

'You like it?' Mel asked her.

Hope nodded, wet-eyed. 'Yes,' she said. 'I like it.'

Sleeping on a spaceship could be a very disconcerting experience, Mel decided.

She had programmed the *Nosferatu II* to follow an Earth-style 24-hour clock, with lighting levels adjusting themselves accordingly. This ship, however, seemed set to permanent day. But she was so tired that she fell asleep only seconds after she lay down on one of the berths in the three-bed room.

How long Mel slept, she had no idea, but she definitely – as her mother used to say – 'felt better for it'. She awoke with renewed determination to crack the *Kazemi*'s computer system. She would have liked a change of clothes and maybe a shampoo, but contented herself with, to use another of her mother's sayings, 'a cat's lick and a promise' in the adjoining washroom, before heading to the flight deck.

Glitz and Hope were both there. As Mel entered, Glitz gave Hope a wink and said, 'Go on, junior – showtime!'

Hope broke into a huge grin. 'Wait there!' she said, with such excitement in her voice that Mel could hardly believe it was the same person who'd been through so much trauma only the day before.

Glitz laughed as Mel raised a quizzical eyebrow. 'I know you are strangely averse to lying,' he said. 'But do please remember that a little white lie never hurt anyone.'

Now what did *that* mean? Why on earth would she need to lie?

She found out soon enough. Hope came back in, carrying a bowl.

'Glitz said you like fruit salad, which is lots of fruits chopped up in pieces all together,' Hope said. With pride on her face, she offered Mel the bowl. Inside were – well, Mel wasn't sure exactly, but taking Earth foods as a template, this resembled chunks of melon and pineapple, halved grapes, a sprinkling of white, orange and red berries ... and pieces of carrot, tomato and (probably the reason Glitz was beaming so widely) chili peppers.

'Goodness,' she said. 'Hope, did you do this yourself?'

The girl nodded. 'Glitz helped a bit. But I picked everything and did the cutting myself.'

Mel was not going to give Glitz the satisfaction of taking the bait. And anyway, she was really touched that Hope had made such an effort.

Maintaining eye contact with Glitz throughout, Mel ate the entire 'fruit salad' – chilis included. It took considerable effort not to pant like a dog, or croak out a desperate plea for water, but she did it.

'Thank you,' she told Hope as she put down her spoon, hardly wheezing at all. 'What a treat.'

Mel managed to keep smiling until Hope left the room to return to the hydroponic garden, then indulged in a mammoth fit of coughing and several pints of recycled water from the galley.

Now she really had to get access to the ship's systems as soon as possible. She wasn't sure if she could eat raw chilis at *every* meal, even to save Hope's feelings ...

After another hour at the computer, things were looking as unpromising as they had the day before. Mel sighed and leaned back in her chair. 'I don't think I can do this,' she told Glitz.

'Admitting defeat, Mel? That's not like you,' said Glitz.

'I'm going to keep trying, of course,' she said. 'But I thought it was only fair to tell you we might be in for rather a long wait. Possibly a *very* long wait.'

'But the *Tu-Two*!' moaned Glitz. 'What will it do without me?' His expression turned to horror. 'What if someone stumbles across it back there? They might think it's abandoned! It could be looted. Seized! Impounded by Deep Space Revenue!'

'I'm sure it'll be OK,' Mel said, but she felt a stab of worry too. The *Nosferatu II* felt like home now. The thought of some pirate – or, yes, even a tax collector – disturbing her impeccably organised storage system ... Ugh.

The awful thought hung over them both for a few moments. Then Glitz said, in a worryingly casual tone, 'So, Mel ...'

'Yes?' she said warily.

'You feel that a solution vis à vis the obtainability of access into the *Kazemi*'s systems will not be immediately forthcoming.'

'That's right,' she said, once she'd deciphered his sentence.

He sighed, and reached into his pocket. Then drew out his hand, empty. 'We could be looking at days, weeks …?'

'Or months, yes. Perhaps longer.'

Glitz once more put his hand in his pocket. Then drew it out again. He looked like a naughty schoolboy who was concealing a recently used catapult behind his back.

'Glitz, are you hiding something?' Mel asked sternly.

'Me? Hiding something? Why would I do that?'

She looked at him, her eyebrows raised high.

Slowly, reluctantly, Glitz put his hand back in his pocket, this time drawing out a small cuboid.

'What's that?' Mel asked.

'"That" is about 10,000 grotzits on the open market,' Glitz said with a groan.

Mel rolled her eyes. 'I meant, what does it do?' She reached out a hand to take it, and Glitz instinctively yanked it out of reach – then with another groan, passed it over to her.

'It's what's known as an AI Interface,' he said. 'I found it back on the supply station. It's like a universal translator, but for computer languages.'

'Why didn't you tell me about it before?' Mel demanded.

'Ten thousand grotzits, Mel!'

Mel had no sympathy whatsoever for Glitz's broken dreams of avarice. 'What does that matter?' she said. 'Grotzits are completely worthless while we're stuck here!'

'You know not what you say!' said a shocked Glitz. 'But I shall forgive your blasphemy against the glorious grotzit and consider it a temporary lapse of judgement while of unsound mind.'

'Unsound mind!' Mel began – but knew this wasn't an argument to pursue. Glitz's love of the grotzit was a tale for the ages. 'How do I use it?'

'Are you absolutely sure you can't get into the computer?' said Glitz, still clearly reluctant. 'This is worth a fortune – it's the Deluxe model!'

Mel looked at it. It was a small yellow cube. In no way did it appear 'deluxe'. 'What does that mean?' she asked.

'It means you don't just get a disembodied voice telling you what to do, you get the full 3D experience. And it's tailored to you, so the thing hasn't even got resale value.'

Mel said again, 'What does that mean?'

'It takes on a humanoid form to interact with you. Specifically, a humanoid form triggered by your own brainwaves; someone you have an emotional connection to, who you see as a mentor or authority figure. So you don't need three guesses to work out who it's going to turn into. In fact, I'd say the maximum you need is *two* guesses.'

'Oh!' said Mel. 'You mean …'

'Yes,' said Glitz with a disgruntled sigh. 'It's going to become the Doctor. Not just look like. Talk like. Act like. *Be* like!'

Chapter Nine

Almost Human

The AI interface was going to look like the Doctor? Mel couldn't work out how to feel.

On the one hand, it would be wonderful to see the Doctor again. It didn't matter that she knew her decision to leave the TARDIS had been the right one; he would always be one of the most important people – probably *the* most important person – in her life. And if it was the old Doctor, the exuberant, curly-haired fanfaron, that would scratch an itch she'd long had: the desire to say a proper farewell before he was ripped from her by the actions of amoral Time Lady the Rani and replaced by the cunning clown whom she liked just as much, but whom she felt – irrationally, she knew – had stolen her first friend from her.

But if the AI was enough like the Doctor to make that meaningful – what else might that mean for her? She'd been so proud of her new independence.

But with the Doctor... she wouldn't be Melanie Bush, she'd become 'the Doctor's friend Mel' – or even just 'the girl' – again. That wasn't who she wanted to be any more. That wasn't who she *was* any more. As far as she was concerned, her days as nothing but a sidekick were gone with the wind.

Something began to ooze from the cube, tendrils of grey that curled into themselves and melted together until they formed a mass – a ball of modelling clay with hands and legs pushing out, as though trying to escape. A featureless head came out of the top, and gradually a humanoid shape pulled itself together, drawing on the ever-oozing tentacles to increase its size. Soon it was up to Mel's knee, then to her waist, but there was no hint yet of any features to indicate its eventual form. Mel thought to herself that if it grew only a few more inches after reaching her height, she'd know which Doctor it would be – if it kept growing until it was taller than Glitz, it was clearly going to be the other one.

It was at her shoulders, at her head – and on it went. It wasn't her friend with the question-mark umbrella and Panama hat, then. It would have been lovely to see that funny old face again – but she felt nothing but happy anticipation as she waited for the Doctor's previous persona to appear.

But the waxen golem crept an inch or two above Glitz's height, and didn't stop for an inch or two more. Mel thought she must just have forgotten how tall her original Doctor was! Colours were swirling on its surface now, oil on water, brilliant yellows and reds – yes, that had to be the earlier Doctor!

The top of the head erupted into curls. But something wasn't right. The clothes now showed silver and gold. The curly hair was dark, not fair, and formed into a vast mass of ringlets that rivalled Mel's own – as well as adding a few inches to the being's height.

But that wasn't the only thing that made it seem so tall; to Mel's amazement a pair of shiny red platform-heeled boots formed at its feet. The Doctor did go in for snazzy footwear, but platform boots? Never.

Who *was* this?

Finally its appearance settled.

This was not the Doctor.

In front of Mel, wearing a glam-rock spacesuit with a Saturn logo on its pocket, a bandana knotted around his lion's mane of hair was …

Barry Day.

Barry Day! The guitarist of Dutch Elm Disease!

Barry Day! Whose face had looked out of posters neatly cut from *Jackie* and *Blue Jeans* and blu-tacked onto Mel's bedroom wall!

Barry Day! The astronomer presenter of *Spaceship Saturday*!

Mel stared and stared and stared. Over the course of her travels with the Doctor she'd encountered many famous faces, but she'd never been left reeling like this before. It was *Barry Day*!

Why had the AI not become the Doctor? Presumably because it must have felt the reservations in her mind as it formed. And she did have an emotional connection to

Barry Day; when she was a child he'd been like a mentor, an authority figure. There was no question that his enthusiasm had contributed to her love for astronomy and technology.

'Mel,' said Glitz, 'what do you get if you cross an astronaut and Louis Quatorze, King of France?'

'I don't know,' said Mel distractedly. 'What do you get if you cross an astronaut and Louis Quatorze, King of France?'

'It wasn't a joke, Mel. I am genuinely interested in your answer.'

Barry Day – no, the AI *impersonating* Barry Day, she had to remember that – gave his famous, heart-stopping lopsided grin, and held out a hand to Glitz. 'Space Agent Barry Day,' he said in the Geordie accent she recalled so well from his TV appearances. 'Thanks for joining us on *Spaceship Saturday*, Sabalom Glitz! This is gonna be space-tacular!'

'Space agent?' said Glitz. 'That doesn't sound even vaguely plausible as a job description. If you're looking for a good cover story, you'll have to do better than that.'

'Barry,' said Mel, stepping in – 'er, do I call you Barry?'

'Course you can, Mel lass,' he said, which wasn't quite answering her question – she wasn't asking for permission, she was more concerned with the correct way to address an AI. Did he *know* he was an AI? Surely he couldn't believe he was the actual Barry Day presenting a children's television programme circa 1980?

'Well, then ... Barry ... Could you help me connect with the ship's computer?'

'That's what I'm here for, lass!'

Well, that was a relief at least. She'd had a sudden terrible vision of having to explain to 'Barry' that, in the words of Pinocchio, he wasn't a real boy.

Barry sat himself at the master console, swinging his platform boots up onto a bank of controls, then correcting himself and putting them back on the floor. 'Mustn't set a bad example,' he hissed in a fake aside to Mel. 'Don't tell Squixy I did that, or … well, you know what'll happen.'

'I do,' hissed back Mel, who couldn't help being sucked into the act a little bit. It was deeply ingrained in every television-watching schoolchild of her generation that you had to be very careful not to do anything that might upset Squixy the Space Squirrel.

'OK, then – let's do this!'

Mel wasn't quite sure what was happening as Barry gestured for her to stand behind him, then guided her hands to either side of his head. She felt a jolt, a strange sensation as though her brain had shifted inside her skull, and then she was looking at the screen …

… through someone else's eyes.

She blinked hard, and was back in her own head again. The code on the screen remained stubbornly indecipherable. But for a moment there …

'Have another go, lassie,' urged Barry.

'Yes, have another go, *lassie*,' echoed Glitz, who had just discovered a whole new raft of things he could tease Mel about in future and was fizzing with happiness at the prospect.

'Am I controlling you?' she asked Barry. 'Or – are you controlling me? What's happening? I'm not sure I like it.'

'I'm just showing you the way in,' he replied. 'Come on, try again. It'll get easier.'

So Mel put her hands either side of his head again, resting her palms against the red bandana. Her brain jolted, and she found herself looking through his eyes once more. As she looked, the characters on the screen morphed into ones she recognised. A sequence she understood. She instinctively began to type on the keypad – and realised it wasn't her hands doing the typing. Instead of her neatly manicured nails, it was Barry's slender, guitar-player's fingers that were touching the keys. The visual disconnect made her jump, returning her to her own head.

'I can't do it,' Mel said. 'It's just too … uncomfortable.'

'What are you talking about?' he said. 'You've already done it. Take a look!'

She looked back – and he was right! She had no problems understanding the code on the screen now. It was a strange, unsettling sensation, though: her eyes and her brain were telling her different things, and she couldn't tell whether it was the same code it had always been, except she could understand it now, or if the images on screen had literally changed into ones she recognised.

Glitz was rubbing his hands. 'Knew that'd work,' he said. 'Brilliant idea of mine. And no –' he put up a hand to stop Mel speaking, although she hadn't shown any indication of doing so – 'I won't hear a word about you paying me back for the extremely valuable AI interface I sacrificed at your request.' He paused, presumably waiting for her protests.

Mel gave him a 'seriously?' look.

Glitz interpreted the look in his own way and carried on: 'No, not a single word. I insist. We'll just take it out of your share of Operation *Tu-Two*'s profits.'

Oh Glitz, never change, Mel thought.

It was actually a pleasant surprise to discover he'd entertained the idea of a profit-share in the first place. In the initial planning stages of their joint venture, there had been no fewer than five occasions where Mel had been 'required' to sign 'essential' documents, only to discover that clumsy, scatterbrained Glitz had accidentally put completely the wrong papers in the middle of the stack – papers that, if signed, would have made Glitz the sole proprietor of not only that business, but any and every venture Mel might pursue in the future. What was especially bizarre was that Glitz didn't have the faintest clue where those papers could have come from! A mischievous creature, possibly a Goblin or a Graske, was his top suspect, or perhaps one of the many, many folk who were envious of his business acumen and success.

'Now we have access to the ship's systems,' said Mel, 'we really have a duty to find out more about the *Kazemi*. There might be all kinds of people somewhere, desperate for news of its fate.' She left Glitz grumbling about how the concept of closure was overrated. He, for example, had no idea what had happened to his father, his mother, his one-time accomplice

Dibber, or any of the three Ogron wives he'd married for tax purposes, and that didn't bother him one bit.

One of the first things Mel found was a crew manifest, a list of ten names and photos. She recognised the faces. She'd seen them on a tapestry in Hope's room on the *Seraphine*.

Mel shuddered as she read through each biog. Knowing these people had ended in the fuel tank was awful, but the more she read, the more they became real people to her, people with hopes and dreams and loves and hates – and oh, that was painful.

And that was a feeling that Glitz, as fond of him as she now was, would never understand. While she imagined the final horrors these poor people had faced, Glitz was pointing out – for example – that Darshim's nose looked like a Shansheeth's beak and that he, Glitz, would have to be paid an Andromedan queen's ransom to take her out to dinner. Mel thought that Darshim, whose biog listed her expertise and qualifications in everything from astrophysics to space medicine, might drive a considerably harder bargain if she were required to spend an evening with Sabalom Glitz, a person who, as he had admitted only a few minutes earlier, had voluntarily married several Ogrons.

Glitz decided that this might be a good time to see how Hope was getting on. He left.

'Is he normally like that?' asked Barry Day.

'Oh yes,' said Mel with a sigh. 'He is.'

She moved on to another folder – and to her surprise, found more crew manifests. She opened the top one. Like the first, it listed ten people. Captain Livyia Terle; Pilot Rufus Kade; First Officer Heide Demarr; Flight Engineer FK Frogmorton; Systems Specialist Rom Bastelle; Life Systems Officer Caleb Havermine; Cook and Quartermaster Triptolemos; Medical Officer TC Nash; Horticulturist Vizhan Xiv; Security Officer Suim Pearleye.

These were as highly qualified as the previous crew, each capable of fulfilling several functions on board ship – the Flight Engineer was also a medic; the First Officer could cook, and so on.

Mel moved on to the next list – another ten people, another roll-call of exceptional talent. Who were they all? Had they died in the *Seraphine*'s tank too? Because they certainly weren't on board the *Kazemi*.

She kept on, examining roster after roster, hypnotised by the endless information, desperate to drag meaning from it. Barry Day sat by her side, giving her a giant grin and telling her she was *space-tacular* every now and again. It was disconcerting, like he didn't exist if she wasn't looking at him, and she was grateful the AI hadn't taken on the form of the Doctor. 'You're doing great!' the Barry simulacrum told her at random intervals.

At last she reached the end of the lists, and had to admit that she was no nearer to finding out more about this ship, or to finding a way to get them off the *Kazemi* and back to the *Nosferatu II*. She was wondering what to look at next, when she spotted a link to another section of the roster. A section labelled ... passengers.

Passengers? There'd not been the slightest sign of any passengers, living or dead. Had they also been victims of the *Seraphine* cult? According to the computer, the ship contained …

Mel stopped. Something had surely been lost in translation. She turned to Barry the AI. 'Can you take a look at this for me?' she said. 'I don't think I can be reading it right.'

'Course you're reading it right, lass!' he said. 'You needed help with the code, not the content. Clear as day – ha!' He laughed. 'Clear as *Barry* Day!' (Oh yes – that had been one of his catchphrases.) '*Kazemi* passenger register: seventy-five million passengers.'

'But … but …' The ship was big, but not 75 million people big – even the giant *Nosferatu II* couldn't carry that many! That was more than the entire population of the United Kingdom at the time she'd left Earth!

Mel did a few quick calculations in her head. If you looked at mass alone and squashed up 75 million average-sized humans so they took up the smallest amount of space possible, you'd still need 62,000 double-decker buses to fit them all in. If there were that many passengers, they had to be the size of fleas! She subconsciously scratched an imaginary itch. Flea-sized. That had to be the answer. A whole population miniaturised or digitised as a way to cross immense distances when space and resources were at a premium. So they were probably here, somewhere, on the ship. Safe inside their tiny world, to return to reality at a later date.

It was one thing planning to return to the *Nosferatu II* and leave a deserted ship floating on forever, it was quite another thing to abandon 75 million people. But what could she do?

'Mel! I've picked some more fruit!' Hope limped onto the flight deck, her arms full of produce.

'Hey, lass!' called Barry Day, before Mel could say anything.

Hope gasped in surprise, and dropped a bunch of tomatoes. They splatted horribly onto the floor, juice, pips and pulp spraying messily across the room.

'Oh no,' called out Barry Day, a long drawn-out cry that sounded more like 'ooooornooooor' – something else Mel remembered well from *Spaceship Saturday*.

And she remembered what always came next, too – but surely that couldn't happen here …?

She was wrong.

Gesturing at the mess on the floor, Barry Day chanted: 'Squixy's gonna go …' and Mel found herself automatically mouthing the last word: 'Nuts!'

She was almost not surprised at all when a space-suited squirrel swooped down in a tiny shuttlecraft and rained a barrage of acorns on them all.

Chapter Ten

Waking the Dead

Mel had been the babysitter of choice for every Pease Pottage parent. She was sensible, practical and polite. She'd completed a first-aid course with the Girl Guides and then done a second course through her own choice in case anything had been missed out of the original one (and had, of course, passed both with flying colours). She was trustworthy, too – everyone knew there was no risk of Melanie Bush sneaking in a forbidden boyfriend, or raiding the drinks cabinet.

Children liked her because she knew a million stories off by heart, could build anything in Lego and was probably the only person in the whole village who could solve a Rubik's Cube in under a minute. In return, Mel enjoyed the feeling of responsibility, as well as the sense of achievement that came with every new computer part she could buy with her wages.

The only blot on the babysitting landscape came when a child decided to push its luck while their usual caregivers were out of the house. They could, they thought, do what they liked with such a soft-hearted, soft-spoken teenager in charge.

Initially, they were right. Mel was left very nearly tearing her hair out after a few nightmarish experiences ...

Until she learned the Voice. Hands on hips, deep breath and—

The Voice.

Things changed, after that. No one who'd heard the Voice would consider her a pushover any more. It wasn't angry. It wasn't shouty. Mel wasn't that sort of person. But oh, it was the voice of authority.

It was the voice that brought naughty pre-schoolers to heel. It was the voice that made seven-year-olds realise that they infinitely preferred colouring books and crayons to graffitiing the walls with their mum's nail varnish.

Now, Mel ducked, shielding her head from the bombardment – then realised she didn't have to. The puppet rodent was still gleefully pelting them all with acorns, but they made no impact. They weren't real!

It was many years since Mel had used the Voice. But it came out of storage, as powerful as ever, when she said: 'Barry – get your squirrel under control.'

It turned out that the Voice worked even on AI interfaces. A shamefaced Barry Day began to – somehow – clean up the illusory acorns as Squixy shot off again.

Mel turned to reassure Hope that the mess wasn't an issue, and found Glitz standing in the doorway staring at her, wide-eyed and open-mouthed. It was probably the first time in their entire acquaintanceship that she'd rendered him speechless. Her announcement that, somewhere, somehow, there were 75 million people on board the *Kazemi* didn't make him bat the slightest eyelid after the shock of the Voice.

But when the effect wore off, so did Glitz's disinterest. 'We're getting out of here, and soon,' he said.

'Why?' Mel asked.

'Seventy-five million is a lot of people, Mel. What are the chances that I haven't ripped off – that is to say, what are the chances that I haven't had non-reciprocally-appreciated business dealings with at least one of them?'

'We're not planning on introducing you to them all individually! I don't even know where on the ship they are.' Mel turned to Barry. 'Can you help me find a plan of the ship?'

'No problem, lass.' Without even going near the computer, he brought up a schematic of the *Kazemi* on a monitor screen. Mel sat down to examine it, Glitz and Hope both looking over her shoulders.

'There's a whole lower level,' she said.

'And it's called the microstore,' said Glitz. 'Miniaturisation may fit the bill here.'

'I think that must be it,' said Mel. 'But I don't think you have to worry about meeting them. I can't even see a way of getting down there. Unless there's another secret door like you found in …' She looked at the plan again. 'That room – it's called the Revival Room. To un-miniaturise people, do you think?'

'You're wrong there, Mel,' said Barry Day, unexpectedly. 'Have another go.'

'Er … I'm not sure,' she said.

'Come on, you can do it! Remember what's at stake.'

'Finding a way back to our ship?'

'Noooooo!' Barry said, dragging out the single syllable. 'Have a think, Mel. You can work it out. You could win the latest LP by ABBA!'

'Oh,' said Mel. 'Um, in that case… There were ten… cavities, would you call them? … in the room, and we found multiple lists of ten people on the computer, so … Oh! How about this? The ship operates with a crew of ten people, but there's a … a rota, if you like. The crews work in shifts! And the crews who aren't on duty are miniaturised – or kept in suspended animation, that would make more sense.' She was on a roll now. 'Remember how the Galactasnax vending machine should have refilled itself, but didn't until Captain Kolahra restored the power? This could be the same. The ship's crew went missing, all ten people, and the *Kazemi* just floated in space for years. The next crew was probably supposed to take over a decade ago, but nothing triggered the revival process. They're still in storage! So that's what we have to do. Find the next crew and wake them up, so they can continue their journey and take the 75 million people to wherever they're supposed to go!'

'Space-tacular!' Barry beamed at her. 'Congratulations, Mel. The LP is yours! Now get your dancing trousers on, lads and lasses, and let's listen to the title track!'

To Mel's utter astonishment, a pop song suddenly blasted out of the flight deck's intercom system.

Hope began to laugh. 'What's this?'

'Um, I think it's "Super Trouper",' said Mel.

Glitz was shaking his head. 'I don't think she means the song title.' He looked at Hope with an almost paternal smile. 'Do you, junior?'

'I mean … this sound!'

Mel gaped. 'Oh! Hope! You've never heard *music* before!' Plants, food, music… Perhaps even *friends*. All new experiences. She gave the girl a hug. 'Like it?'

'This "music"? I *love* it!'

Barry Day began to dance. Mel had forgotten that dance! Awkward, limbs sticking out all over the place, but just… happy. Squixy had appeared again, and she too was dancing, waving her paws from side to side, as though a puppeteer's hand was controlling her from behind the computer console she perched on.

Hope started to copy their movements, and her sheer joie de vivre showed in every twirl. As the song ended, Squixy beckoned to Hope and presented her with a badge. Mel knew without looking what it would say on it: SQUIXY'S SPACE SQUAD.

Hope had just won a Squixy's Space Squad badge.

Hope was now part of Squixy's Space Squad!

127

'Oh!' said Mel. 'I always wanted to win a Squixy badge!' But she didn't begrudge it to Hope in the slightest. The girl's happiness was almost tangible.

Hope laughed. 'I feel like … I feel like I've been asleep all my life and suddenly I'm awake!'

Awake. That took Mel out of the moment. 'That's wonderful, Hope. Now we have to find out how to wake up the next crew.'

'Whoa-whoa-whoa! Hold on to your horses, Melanie.' Glitz was shaking his head. 'We've got access to the system now thanks to Mr Saturday Starship over there, but first let's get a shuttle up and running in case things turn nasty.'

'*Spaceship Saturday*,' Mel corrected and added, 'Isn't that a bit paranoid?'

Glitz raised his eyebrows. 'I know you like to think the best of everyone, Mel, but can I remind you that earlier today we were almost sacrificed to feed the belly of a rusty space vessel? Paranoia and staying alive are just two sides of the same coin.'

Barry turned to an invisible camera. 'We have a request here from Sabalom Glitz of Salostopus. It's an oldie but a goody! Here you go, Sabalom!'

'Stayin' Alive' by the Bee Gees suddenly burst out of the speakers.

'Not the time, Barry,' Mel said, her tone edging close to the Voice again. The music shut off. Hope looked disappointed.

'OK, Mel, we're gonna take a break now,' Barry said. 'But make sure you stick around – we've got interviews with all ten members of the newly awakened Crew D coming up later, and it's gonna be space-tacular!'

'What?' Mel gasped.

'You know, lass! Just as you ordered. "Wake up the next crew, so they can continue their journey and take the 75 million people to wherever they're supposed to go."'

'That wasn't an order!' Barry didn't react. 'Oh, never mind. Glitz, we'd better get to the Revival Room.'

'No, we'd better get to the *shuttle*! Tell the laughing cavalier there to add us to the system, now!'

'No can do,' said Barry. 'Sorry, Sabalom. Wish I could help, but only crewmembers can use the shuttles.'

'Then make us crewmembers, you frizzy-haired fool!'

Barry grinned up at the non-existent camera. 'Coming up — it's a race against time! Can Mel, Hope and Sabalom complete the rigorous six-month training process to join the crew of the *Kazemi* before Crew D wake up? What d'you reckon, Squixy?'

'Squeak squeak!'

'Yeah, you're right. It'll be a hard nut to crack. But we believe in them!'

Mel shook her head in resignation. 'Come on,' she told the others. 'Looks like we're going to the Revival Room after all.'

They'd left the entrance open, so there was no need to force their way in this time.

The shallow box with its ten empty cavities was still the only thing in the room.

Were the new crewmembers just going to appear in it?

It was Hope who first noticed what was happening. 'Look!' she said. 'It's moving!'

She was right. The structure was rising off the ground.

'Now that,' said Barry Day with a laugh, 'is what I'd call out of this world!'

Mel had thought of a candle mould when she'd first seen the box and, in a roundabout way, she'd not been too far off the mark.

Not candlewax, but beeswax.

What she'd thought of as a box was more like a frame, the sort found in beehives. As a beekeeper would slide out a frame from the hive, brushing off the clinging bees to see the honeycomb below before sliding it back in and repeating the process, so here the original frame had slid back into a 'hive' structure above them, and a second frame was now being brought down. The frames fitted so seamlessly into the ceiling that a casual glance upwards had shown no indication of their existence.

The second frame had ten cavities, just like the previous one. There was something inside each cavity, but those somethings were hidden by some viscous liquid in electric pink.

'Oooooornooooooor!' cried Barry Day. 'They've been gunged! Squixy, did you do that?'

'Squeak!' The squirrel shook her head, but Mel had to admit that – whatever the stuff was – it did look *exactly* like Squixy's galaxy gunge.

The ooze slowly drained away. Ten figures were revealed, sticky with pink; sodden hair painted on to their skulls; damp jumpsuits clinging to torso and limbs.

Mel felt uncomfortably like a voyeur as she watched this process, but she had to stay.

Hope wavered between nervousness and excitement. Squixy had moved from Barry's shoulder to Hope's, and would lean in to hug her whenever the nerves seemed to be winning.

Glitz seemed irritated and impatient. As well as wanting to get away, Mel knew that he'd probably been imagining a future in which the entirety of the *Kazemi*, every last component of its infrastructure, each accoutrement and appurtenance of the 'abandoned' ship, passed into his possession. Or rather, passed into his possession very briefly, before being passed into someone else's possession in exchange for an extremely large pile of grotzits. That future was definitely off the table now.

Clear liquid splashed down into the leftmost chamber and washed the goop away. A tall, slender woman with short dark hair was revealed. 'Here we go!' said Barry Day. 'It's Livyia Terle, age at commencement 36. She doesn't mind friends calling her Livyia, but when it's worktime, you call her Captain Terle. Yes – Livyia's captain of the ship! How cool is that, lads and lasses? You know what – girls can do anything! Isn't that right, Squixy?'

'Squeak squeak,' Squixy agreed. Barry winked at Mel and gave her a thumbs up.

Livyia was blinking, still not fully awake, as Barry moved on to the next person. This was a man, clean-shaven and athletic-looking. Barry's introduction informed them this was Rufus Kade, pilot, whose age at commencement had been 23.

The introductions continued down the line as each crewmember was revealed.

Waist-length platinum blonde hair, tall, curvy and striking: that was Heide Demarr, First Officer, age at commencement 34.

Petite, shaven head: FK Frogmorton, the flight engineer, age at commencement 28, noted to be commonly called 'Frog'.

Stocky, brown hair and beard, and probably no taller than Mel: that was Rom Bastelle, systems specialist, age at commencement 31.

Tall and muscular, square-jawed and side-burned: Caleb Havermine, life systems officer, age at commencement 24.

Gangly, with bald head and a goatee: unmistakably Triptolemos, the cook and quartermaster, age at commencement 39.

Slender brunette with dark eyes and cheekbones to die for: that was TC Nash the medical officer, age at commencement 26.

Tall and dark-haired, could almost be the captain's kid sister: Vizhan Xiv, horticulturist, age at commencement 24.

Silvering hair and deep-set eyes: that was Suim Pearleye, in charge of security, age at commencement 41.

By the time Barry had reached Pearleye, Captain Livyia Terle was fully awake – and not looking happy. Mel glanced at her two companions and decided she would have to be the grown-up here.

She stepped forward.

'Hello,' she said to the captain. 'I expect you're wondering what's going on here ...'

The reception that Mel and the others received from Crew D was considerably better than expected. While saddened by the loss of their predecessors, the teammates showed no animosity towards Hope for her unwitting part in the tragedy. They expressed their appreciation to Mel in particular for wanting to do the right thing for the *Kazemi* and those on it.

It was imperative for each crewmember to go to their workstation and make an urgent assessment of the state of the ship and its journey, but the captain assured Mel that they would make arrangements regarding a return to the *Nosferatu II* as soon as possible. She admitted that she was unlikely to approve an additional trip in the *Kazemi* – they had so much time to make up! – but was not necessarily averse to letting them have a shuttle. She would consult with systems specialist Bastelle, and endeavour to find a solution that worked for everyone.

Then the captain, Kade, Demarr and Caleb went to the flight deck; Bastelle, Pearleye and Frog went to the engine room; Triptolemos went to the galley; Nash went to the medical centre and Vizhan went to the hydroponic garden. Mel was invited to the flight deck, and Glitz indicated an interest in checking out the engine room.

Hope, with Squixy swinging on one of her pigtails, asked to go with him.

It was clear, almost from the moment they'd been revived, that the crew had a real rapport. Listening to Livyia, Kade, Demarr and Caleb talking, Mel realised why.

The six months of training that Barry had mentioned were only the tip of the iceberg; psychological evaluations had been used to carefully craft crews that should work in complete harmony, which were then tested to their limits in a number of trials. Not only were all ten therefore well acquainted before the journey began, this was their sixth tour of duty – they'd previously spent five separate years working together on the *Kazemi*.

Livyia Terle was authoritative but with a very gentle way of speaking. If she gave an order, the others acted like it was their privilege to be able to carry it out.

Kade, the pilot, had a cheeky grin and kept ribbing the stolid life-systems officer Caleb.

Heide Demarr, although pleasant, seemed a very intense person – Mel felt immediately comfortable with the other three, but wasn't quite sure how to act around Demarr.

Mel had hoped to help out on the flight deck, but ended up just doing her best to keep out of everyone's way. The crew's job titles didn't do justice to the size of their responsibilities. Anything to do with the journey was dealt with by Kade.

External repairs and maintenance came under Frog's purview; for internal matters Demarr was in charge. Bastelle was the computer expert, controller of the ship's system. Caleb maintained the microstore, continually monitoring it from a console on the flight deck. Triptolemos dealt with all domestic matters, as well as food and supplies. Pearleye's title of 'Security' included responsibility for the crew's wellbeing. And the captain was in overall charge of all of the above, and absolutely everything else too. So, what Mel mainly did while the crew rushed purposefully around, was listen.

It was then that she learned about the custom of the welcome meal.

Each retiring crew left behind a meal consisting of a particular spicy vegetable dish called gercaplis, which was made with ship-grown produce, served with flatbreads and a type of pickle that took several months to mature, and a baked fruit tart made with fresh berries. Meals eaten at other times were much simpler, so it was symbolic that the previous crew would choose to spend time and resources on providing this meal for their successors, not for themselves. The two crews would never meet, but this formed a bond between them, a showing of respect for the fellow guardians of their mission.

Of course Crew D understood why there was no welcome meal this time, but Mel could see that it was a hit to morale, on top of the huge knock they'd already taken.

Maybe she could be useful after all!

True, despite being a fan of healthy eating, she wasn't exactly an experienced chef. 'Why not give it a go!' had, though, always been one of Mel's mottos.

Mel knew that her enthusiasm sometimes overwhelmed her tact. So, when she visited Triptolemos in the galley, she was careful to say that she was sure he was capable of making a wonderful meal for everyone. But she would like to welcome Crew D by providing – as much as she could – a taste of home.

Well, *her* home. A taste of Pease Pottage, circa 1986 …

Chapter Eleven

The Killing

'Morning, everyone! Here we are in the Cosmic Kitchen, with our special guest, Melanie Bush! Hey, Mel – who eats nuts and bolts?'

'I don't know, Barry. Who eats nuts and bolts?'

'Squixy in a hurry!'

The puppet squirrel sat on Barry's shoulder and squeaked a laugh. Mel laughed too.

'Now, Mel, I understand you want to make a meal that's ... space-tacular!'

'That's the idea, Barry!'

'So tell us – what's on the menu?'

'We're doing melon to start – well, a fruit that's a bit like melon, anyway – followed by a sort of nut roast with salad, and then a berry trifle to finish. Oh, and carrot cocktail to drink.'

'Champion!'

'*Squeak* squeak?'

'You heard right, Squixy! Nut roast! I'm sure Mel will save a portion for you.'

'Of course I will, Squixy.'

Mel didn't exactly have all the ingredients she needed for her menu, but her memory had pulled together information from various sources – recipe books, cookery shows, home economics lessons – and worked out what she hoped were good substitutions. She was confident – well, pretty confident – well, fairly confident – that it would turn out well.

'Squeak? Squeak squeak squeak squeak-squeak squeak-squeak squeak squeak squeak-squeak?'

'What's that, Squixy? Where does a pirate squirrel keep his treasure? Mel?'

'I don't know, Squixy. Where does a pirate squirrel keep his treasure?'

'Squeak squeak *squeak*-squeak!'

'In a chest-nut! Geddit?'

Mel got it – and laughed. 'You're a class act, Squixy!' She was slightly ashamed of herself, but when working up the menu she had chosen dishes that might appeal to a squirrel – would that be enough to earn her a place in Squixy's Space Squad...?

... which was a ridiculous goal. Because this wasn't *Spaceship Saturday*, and the gorgeous guy who kept pushing a microphone at her was *not* guitarist-turned-astronomer-turned-TV-presenter Barry Day, he – *it* – was merely a three-dimensional artificial intelligence. It was capable of mimicking the character it had found inside her mind and, presumably because it was the deluxe model, it did that extremely well – but that was all it was. She needed to concentrate on what was important – the meal might create enough good feeling to get them a shuttle back to the *Nosferatu II*. 'Barry,' she said. 'Would you mind... waiting outside the galley? So I can concentrate on the cooking.'

Barry smiled that incredible lopsided grin, and Mel had to mentally give herself a very quick but very stern talking-to. 'Please,' she said. 'Just for a bit.'

'Well,' he said, 'I'm supposed to stick with you, lass. Got a sort of link, you know. But you could always pause me for an hour or two.'

How did you *pause* a *person*? No. Not a person. Even when he smiled at her like that, this AI was not Barry Day. 'How do I do that?' she asked. 'Do I just say, "Barry, pause for a couple of hours", or something?'

Barry didn't reply.

'Barry, how do I...'

His grin became even more lopsided – as though it was melting. As she watched, Barry Day dissolved until he – it – was just a small yellow cube again. Mel picked it up and put it in her pocket. She really had to remember that the AI sometimes took her words as commands...

But it definitely was easier to get on with the job at hand without a TV presenter trying to interview her for his non-existent audience.

Triptolemos had happily contributed various packages of store cupboard ingredients, but the fresh produce that Hope had gathered earlier wasn't enough to feed the whole crew – and as the 'special' fruit salad was definitely not part of the menu, a different selection of produce was required. Mel went to look for Hope to ask her to help collect some more.

But Hope wasn't in the engine room with Glitz. 'A touch of discomfort in her wounded limb,' he told Mel. 'Mr Bastelle escorted her to the onboard sawbones.'

'That's Nash, isn't it?' Mel asked. 'OK, I'll go to the medical centre. See if she's there.'

As Mel approached the medical centre, she heard raised voices and quickened her pace. 'Is everything all right?' she asked on arrival, aiming the question at Hope, who looked extremely uncomfortable.

'Just some … crossed wires,' said Bastelle.

'No crossed wires!' The horticulturist, Vizhan, was wearing an expression that Mel would describe as 'peeved'. 'I need to make a solution of spiniphids for the garden; the winterberries are drowning in spong-rot. Nash has some …'

'That stays in the medical centre,' Nash said. 'For now at least. It's human grade, not plant grade.'

'Oh dear,' said Mel. 'I was rather hoping I could have some produce for the kitchen, but if there's spong-rot …'

'See? My fruit and vegetables are *needed*!' Vizhan went from irritated to beaming instantly. 'It's only the winterberries. You can have anything else. I shall happily give this young lady a little tour and we'll pick things together. OK?'

'OK,' said Hope, smiling back.

'OK,' echoed Mel. 'That'd be great. 'Don't take too long, though – there's a lot of preparation to do!'

Mel had finished all the measuring and mixing she could manage by the time Hope came running into the galley. With her bad leg buckling, she looked like Bambi dancing on ice – or a teenage Hansel or Gretel, dropping fruit and vegetables in place of breadcrumbs to create a trail as she ran.

'Are these all right?' the girl asked, unloading the remainder of the produce onto a kitchen bench.

'Perfect!' said Mel. She separated out the almost-carrots. 'Could you cut these up ready for juicing?' Mel herself took on the sorting of the salad vegetables. That just left the melon-like fruits, which needed to be cut and deseeded, and a smiling Triptolemos handled that job.

Ingredients finally prepared, Mel set to work to magic them into something that might, if you squinted from a distance, be amazing.

Triptolemos wielded an enthusiastic cleaver, splitting melon-fruits in two as Mel made short work of tomatoes and vegetables for the salad. 'This will be stupendous!' he cried. 'Marvellous! Gercaplis? Pickles? Pft! They will be forgotten – yes, forgotten! – with the first taste of nut roast. When it is time for Crew E, I will leave for them a note: it will say, "No gercaplis for you! Instead here is something so much better – Melanie's nut roast and trifle!"'

'I think you might be overestimating my cookery skills,' Mel said. 'This won't be anywhere near as good as you could make, Triptolemos. It's just a friendly gesture, that's all.'

'Because we are all friends! Yes, that is so. You, Mel, are my friend, and little Hope there, she is my friend, and ...'

Mel looked up – why had he trailed off? The gregarious cook's face had gone blank. A bad memory? Then his cleaver slammed down again, hard, setting the melon halves rocking.

But the moment passed almost before it had begun, and Triptolemos was laughing and joking with them again.

The food was nearly ready, and Mel felt a surge of happiness as she and Hope laid the table in the crew room. In this age of Galactasnax and nutripills, it wasn't just the food but the ritual that stirred something inside her. Just as she and Glitz had grown closer by meeting up in the ice-cream parlour to swap stories of their day, so would the *Kazemi*'s crew bond by breaking bread together. (Of course, there was no actual bread. As Mel had realised earlier, it might be considered a very basic foodstuff where she came from, but it wasn't easy to make in space.)

There were ten seats at the table – four along each side, and one each at either end. But it was a generous size, and Mel didn't have any difficulty fitting in another three. Thirteen at dinner! It was lucky she wasn't superstitious.

In ones and twos, the crew filed in once they'd finished their most urgent work tasks. Glitz had an arm draped over Pearleye's shoulder, giving him the hard sell about how this or that was exactly the thing he needed to make his life considerably better, and available from Glitz at a very reasonable price.

Mel had Vizhan on her right and Rom Bastelle on her left. Triptolemos took charge of serving the meal. As the plates were passed down the table, each recipient was so extravagant with their praise that Mel felt quite embarrassed. 'You haven't even tried it yet!' she kept saying.

'If it's as good as this carrot cocktail it'll be a feast!' said Kade, the pilot, and everyone else cheered.

Mel thought she couldn't get any more embarrassed until some extremely strange sounds started emanating from … her? Mel shrieked and pushed her chair back, grabbing the yellow cube from her pocket and throwing it onto the floor – where it grew once more into the silver-jumpsuited, platform-shoed figure of Barry Day.

'Hey, lass! That's your two hours of pause complete.' He looked at the table, and Mel realised she hadn't set a place for him – well, why would she? He wasn't *real*! But she still felt awkward about it.

'There's room for another chair here,' said Vizhan, obviously noticing Mel's expression. She indicated a gap on her right. 'Please, come sit with me.'

'Space-tacular!' said Barry, and everyone squashed up, making another place at the table.

'Hey, Trip, I reckon your job's in danger!' Kade the pilot called across the table to Triptolemos, and then to Bastelle, next to the cook. 'Don't you go adding them to the system just yet.' He leaned towards Hope, who was sitting next to him. 'You're not going to be needing a shuttle, we're gonna persuade you all to stay with us!'

Mel glanced at Glitz and Hope and smiled awkwardly. 'Lovely though that offer is, we're looking forward to getting out of your hair, and back to our ship.'

'Not in one of our shuttles, though!' That wasn't from Kade, but from the petite engineer, Frog. There was a laugh in her voice that suggested it was a joke – but Mel knew it wasn't.

Others picked up on it too. 'What d'you mean, Frog?' asked Pearleye, who sat beside her. 'Why not?'

The engineer shrugged. 'We've lost one of our shuttles. We can't afford to lose the other one.'

'We'd still be in the deep freeze if it wasn't for these folk!' said Bastelle. 'We owe them.'

'We owe more to our people!' Caleb put in. 'The future of our entire race is at stake here. Seventy-five million outweighs four, however grateful we might be. So don't you go adding them to the system, Bastelle.'

Mel didn't think this was a good place to point out that there were only three of them – Barry Day, sitting on the far side of Viz with his plate untouched in front of him, didn't count.

'We will save this discussion for later.' Livyia Terle, at the head of the table, rose slightly from her seat for emphasis. 'We owe Mel, Glitz and Hope a debt that must be paid – but everyone's points of view will be taken into account.'

Mel looked over at Glitz as the captain sat back down again. There might well be a 'told you so' coming Mel's way in the not-too-distant future. But Mel's sense of right and wrong would never have let her abandon all the people on this ship, and Glitz was well aware of that.

Vizhan changed the subject. 'This is what's eaten on your home planet, Mel?'

'More or less,' Mel said, grateful for the distraction. 'My cooking isn't exactly at gourmet level, but it ranks above school dinners, at least.'

'School dinners?'

'Splodges of food on a tray. We had spam a lot, or corned beef. Everything came with cabbage or custard. Sometimes the custard was pink.' She laughed. 'I'd better not say too much more about custard until you've tasted the trifle!'

The trifle had been tasted (and admired) when awkwardness flared up again – and again, Frog was responsible, claiming that Heide Demarr, who as First Officer sat at the foot of the table, was monopolising the conversation of medical officer Nash who sat between them.

The normally soft-spoken Vizhan raised her voice to speak over them. 'Would you like some more to drink, Mel?' she said, picking up a jug.

'What exactly is in this "carrot cocktail"?' Glitz enquired, leaning across the table and scrutinising the liquid.

Mel gave a slight cough. 'Well – carrot juice, of course.'

'And the bit that makes it a cocktail is …?'

'That I put a sprig of mint on the top?'

Glitz shook his head. 'May you be forgiven, Melanie. Luckily I have a flask of gwampa juice in my pocket ...' He drew out a silver bottle and added some to his goblet.

'It's very rude not to share,' Mel murmured. Glitz looked at her. She looked back. Perhaps remembering the Voice, Glitz decided that in the spirit of friendship, and for absolutely no other reason, he would pass around his flask to top up each person's glass with a tot of gwampa juice – a delicacy that produced a sensation rather like drinking popping candy and left your tongue tingling for a good half hour afterwards.

Squixy hopped over and pretended to take a sip from Mel's glass. She then got (presumably pretend) hiccups. 'Go and drink a glass of water backwards,' Mel hissed at the squirrel. 'I think the captain's about to make a speech.' Squixy looked sulky. 'Sorry,' Mel whispered, 'but we've got to keep on her good side.'

Captain Terle stood up. 'Colleagues and friends – and new friends.' With those words, the captain indicated Mel, Glitz, Hope and, after an almost imperceptible pause, Barry and Squixy. 'I wish our sixth awakening did not have to begin with such sadness. We mourn the loss of Crew C. Our journey is long, and we who are privileged to have been chosen as guardians of our people know that we will not live to see our destination. We have accepted that as a price we are willing to pay, for through it we ensure the future we all desire. Yet although a life may be willingly given, its theft is still a crime. We will remember their names.'

She listed the ten names then raised her goblet.

All present echoed her toast.

'Before we all return to our duties, let us say thank you to Mel for producing this wonderful welcome meal for us all. I know her generosity will live long in our memories. To Mel!'

Mel was embarrassed, but couldn't deny she was pleased too. 'I'm just very glad you enjoyed it,' she said, when they had toasted her.

'Yes, if this is the food on your planet, I would like to visit!' Vizhan said, as everyone fell back into conversation with their nearest neighbours. 'Do you go home often?'

'It's complicated,' Mel said at last. 'I probably haven't been *properly* home for a year or two.'

'You miss it?'

Another awkward question. She'd already acknowledged that the day-to-day life of Pease Pottage wasn't for her. But there were things she missed about it, of course. She might have been unfulfilled in many ways, but that wasn't the same as being unhappy.

'Yes,' she told Vizhan. 'Yes, there are things that I miss.'

'Like school dinners?'

'Not like school dinners! Those are far in my past, at least!' She laughed. 'I'm happy where I am. But I expect I will go back to Earth one day, even if just for a visit—'

Vizhan barked, 'Earth?' in a tone of pure surprise. 'How can you be from Earth?'

'You know it, then?' asked Mel, worried that the conversation was about to get difficult.

'Of course! We are from Earth. Don't you know? How can you not know? There is no Earth any more. Earth is gone, it vanished!'

Yes, this was definitely going to be awkward.

'I just need a top-up,' Mel said, reaching for the jug of carrot juice. She poured herself a glass, and served some to Vizhan too, as a way to buy time.

She was aware that in this time period, the Earth and its whole constellation had been dragged billions of miles across space, and that the movement had created a fireball that devastated the planet – a planet that had been renamed Ravolox.

It was actually on Ravolox that the Doctor and Glitz had first met, and Mel herself had been present when the Doctor discovered the truth behind what had happened.

But – perhaps because she hadn't seen the devastation for herself – there'd always been a disconnect in her mind between her thoughts of Earth and the knowledge of what had happened to it. To her, the Earth was the Earth, and it would always exist as such – even if she knew that didn't exactly mesh with reality right now.

But explaining this to Vizhan – or any of the crew – was not going to be easy. She hadn't been sworn to secrecy over the Ravolox revelations, but did she have the right to tell them what she knew?

She glanced over at Glitz, who was deep in conversation with Pearleye. She needed to talk to him; he had more experience with this sort of thing.

'I'm so sorry,' she said to Vizhan. 'I just need to speak to my partner for a moment. Glitz?' she called across the table. 'Could I have a quick word, please?'

'In a minute, Mel. I'm just explaining to my good friend Mr Pearleye here the remarkable benefits of—'

'Now would be better,' Mel insisted. She walked round the table to him, and took his elbow. 'Sorry, it's urgent. Won't keep him long,' she told Pearleye, as she practically dragged Glitz to his feet and led him out of the room.

'You're not usually this desperate for my company, Mel!' said Glitz, when they were halfway down the corridor.

'It's not your company, it's your advice I need,' she told him. 'I've just found out that the *Kazemi* comes from Earth!'

'I'd say that was fairly obvious from the beginning,' said Glitz. 'Space Invaders?'

'They're from space, they could be invading anywhere!'

'Well, how many places in the universe have tomatoes?'

'There are lots of planets where people look human!' Mel said. 'I thought it might be the same with tomatoes!'

'Of course.' Glitz smote his forehead. 'The universal tomato.'

'It's not that far-fetched! I mean, we get carrots on the *Tu-Two!*'

'And do you know the effort I have to go to, to procure them?'

'You ... import the carrots?'

'And I don't begrudge it for one moment.'

'Why do you—'

There was a shout from back in the crew room, but Mel couldn't make out the words. Her instinct was always to head to those in need, and she reflexively turned back. But no – there were eleven people and an AI Interface in the crew room to deal with whatever the problem was, and she hadn't even begun to ask Glitz about the ins and outs of the Ravolox situation, so …

There was another shout. And this time she understood the words. They were: 'Ooooornoooor! Squixy's gonna go …' And once again, she felt herself reflexively completing the sentence: 'nuts.'

Someone screamed.

Mel and Glitz looked at each other, then ran – Mel towards the sound, Glitz away from it.

Hope met her in the doorway, and threw herself into Mel's arms. The tableau Mel glimpsed over the girl's shoulder was grotesque in its mixture of horror and ridiculousness.

She could see someone slumped face-down on the table. Nash was leaning over the prone figure, with Livyia Terle by their side. People were looking on as the squirrel shuttle zoomed overhead, dispensing acorn bombs on to the table.

'Squixy *really* doesn't like it when someone gets murdered,' commented Barry. 'But here's a good one: Why didn't Squixy inherit her dead aunt's estate? Because it was en*tailed*!'

Mel gaped at him. She felt she'd stumbled into another dimension. 'Someone's dead?' she cried. 'What happened?' She realised with horror that the prone figure was Vizhan. She'd been talking to her only moments ago!

A rather sheepish-looking Glitz now joined her – presumably having realised there was nowhere to run to. Mel moved Hope very gently aside, nudging her into Glitz's care, and entered the room. 'Is she ...?' she began, but it was a pointless question. 'Can I – can I do anything?' she asked instead.

'I think you've already done enough,' said Frog.

'What do you mean?' asked Mel.

'Well, it looked like you and Vizhan were having an argument. You put something in her glass then you left the room – and now she's dead.'

'But – it wasn't an argument! And I didn't put anything in her glass – I mean, I did, but it was just carrot juice, you all had some ...' Then it registered exactly what they were saying. 'You think she was poisoned? And that I did it?' She held out her hands, palms up – there had to be a way to convince them that she was innocent, but she couldn't think straight. She just kept looking at the body that only minutes before had been a living person. 'I know you don't know me, but I promise you, I could never hurt anyone – never!'

'It's true,' said Glitz, who'd moved to stand behind her and put a protective hand on her shoulder. 'Mel here is ridiculously, painfully honest. She's such a good person that bad guys get an allergic reaction from being in the same room as her. It's been less than twenty-four Earth-standard hours since she last offered to sacrifice her own life to save someone else, which is a thing she has done on many previous occasions, although no one has as yet taken her up on it. If you look up the word "paragon" in the dictionary, the definition says: "Melanie Bush".'

Mel was simultaneously touched and embarrassed. 'Um … that's probably enough,' she whispered. Then, in case he was being genuine, added, 'But thank you.'

'I'm a salesman, Mel,' he whispered back. 'Got to lay it on thick!' He leaned forward and hissed in her ear again. 'We need to get that shuttle. You know how these things go. The strangers are the problem. If I had a grotzit for every time I've been accused of a crime, I'd be a very wealthy man.'

'How rich would you be if you got a grotzit every time you'd been *wrongly* accused of a crime, though?' asked Mel.

'That's irrelevant,' said Glitz. 'And this time, I happen to be innocent.'

This time, Mel noted.

But she believed him. Committing crime came as naturally as breathing to Glitz, but he didn't do it without reason. And not only did he have no reason for killing Vizhan, it had clearly done their cause no good at all – which he would have known to be a consequence.

The captain called for quiet. 'I know we are all deeply shocked by what's happened here, but Mel has shown us nothing but kindness. Please refrain from accusations until we know more.'

'But none of *us* would have killed Vizhan!' shouted Frog.

'How do you know it's murder?' asked Mel desperately.

In answer, Nash moved away from the table, revealing Vizhan's face.

It was horribly contorted, as though Vizhan were emitting a silent scream. Mel had to face the awful truth: it really didn't look like a natural death.

'But that doesn't mean one of us killed her!' she insisted.

'Who else could it be?' Frog shouted. 'There's us and you, and it wasn't us!'

'Frog, calm down,' said Livyia.

But Frog wasn't cowed. 'Captain, our responsibility is to the 75 million people in the microstore. You have the authority to execute anyone that might threaten their wellbeing.'

Mel gasped. *Execute?*

'I also have the authority to determine what is or is not a threat to our people's wellbeing,' the captain said. 'And at the moment, I am not prepared to class Mel, or Glitz, or Hope as an immediate threat.'

'But isn't it better to be safe than sorry—' Frog began.

Livyia cut across her, and this time there was enough authority in her tone to halt Frog in her tracks. 'I am not sanctioning the killing of anyone right now,' she said. 'We are not Chicago mobsters, we are officers of Earth.' She looked round the table. 'Crew D, we have matters to discuss. Mel, Glitz, Hope – perhaps you'd like to explore the facilities in the recreation room?'

Mel nodded. It was an obvious dismissal. 'Come on, Glitz,' she said.

'So, who's the murderer?' asked Barry in a spooky voice. 'Send in your answers on a postcard, addressed to

Spaceship Saturday, care of the *Kazemi*, Somewhere in Space, and we'll pick a winner next week. One lucky viewer will get a Squixy Goes Nuts T-shirt, a front-row seat for the killer's execution, and the latest Adam and the Ants LP!'

'Barry,' said Mel. 'I need you to pause. Now!'

Chapter Twelve
Prime Suspect

Mel, Glitz and Hope were in the rec room. Glitz had parked himself in the comfiest chair and closed his eyes. Mel envied his ability to relax at times like this. Her anxiety increased when Caleb and Pearleye joined them. They were apparently 'just having some downtime', but Mel doubted it was coincidence that the two biggest members of the crew felt a sudden need to unwind away from the others. They were clearly keeping the three newcomers under guard.

Less than an hour ago, Livyia had given a speech calling Mel, Glitz and Hope their 'new friends' and everyone had drunk Mel's health.

And now...

Mel didn't plan to just sit around while the crew decided whether or not to trust them. For now, she knew they must assume – as everyone else seemed to have done already – that Vizhan had been poisoned.

Murdered.

They were in the middle of a real-life whodunnit, where finding the killer might be the only thing that could save their lives.

How might poison have been given to Vizhan? Food or drink seemed the most obvious culprits, but everyone had consumed the same things at the same time.

Or had they ...? Mel suddenly remembered that moment in the garden where Glitz had seemed reluctant to try a grape.

'Hope!' she said, excited. 'When you were picking fruit and veg in the hydroponic garden, did you see Vizhan eat anything?'

The girl shook her head. 'No ... no, I don't think so. But I could have missed it. Why?'

'Everything in there's overgrown. After all, it'd been left to itself for over a decade. I'm not saying the plants have evolved into something dangerous, and I've been *there*, believe me.' She shuddered. 'I'm not talking about killer cucumbers or sentient celery or anything like that. We know there's spong-rot – whatever that is. So I'm thinking that maybe something just ... became rotten. Or the water supply was contaminated, or their nutrient source. Things like salad leaves and melons carry a high risk of food poisoning – people on Earth have died from eating them.'

'Do people really die from eating food?' asked Holly, sounding concerned. 'I thought food was nice. Much nicer than Galactasnax.'

'It doesn't happen often,' said Mel. 'But it can, if people aren't careful, or if they have an allergy. I know we've eaten a lot of things out of the garden, but maybe we were just lucky and Vizhan wasn't.'

Caleb and Pearleye were competing against each other at the arcade-style Space Invaders machine, but it was clear that they'd been listening in the whole time. 'You wouldn't die that quickly from food poisoning,' Pearleye said.

'Maybe it's some super-evolved strain of bacteria!' said Mel. She glanced over at Glitz, hoping for some support, but he gave a suspiciously obvious snore. 'I don't know, I'm just trying to find a way to show that Vizhan wasn't murdered. You see, you and your crew are like family, chosen because you work in perfect harmony with each other. That means you're sure none of you would hurt Vizhan, so you think one of us must be to blame instead. But I know for a fact that Glitz, Hope and I aren't guilty. So I also know that there must be another explanation. And this could be it. It's got to be worth checking out, at least?'

Pearleye and Caleb exchanged glances.

'All right,' Caleb said at last. 'I'll ask Nash to collect some samples from the garden to examine.'

Pearleye nodded. 'I'll go and let the captain know.'

Mel gave them both a huge, relieved smile. 'Thank you!' she said.

They nodded, and left the room. The suddenly-no-longer-sleeping Glitz immediately jumped up and went to follow them – but the door was shut in his face.

'Hey!' he said, as they heard the lock fasten from the other side.

Mel grimaced. 'I suppose it was too much to ask that they believe us straight away,' she said, 'but at least they didn't just dismiss the idea. The captain seems like a very fair person, so—'

'So she'll make sure we have a proper trial before we're executed?'

Hope started to cry. 'This is all my fault!'

'No it isn't!' Mel assured her, glaring at Glitz.

'If I'd understood what Finrae was doing back on the *Seraphine*—' Hope wailed.

'You wouldn't have been able to do anything about it! He had everyone under his spell.'

'But perhaps he was right! I should have stayed behind. My destiny was there. Not here.'

Mel hugged the girl. 'Your destiny is to be whatever you want to be. I'm glad you're here. And we're going to work it all out. We'll—'

She broke off. She was looking over Hope's shoulder, and a porthole was in her direct line of vision.

Something was out there.

Something was moving...

Mel patted Hope on the arm and let her go. She hurried over to the porthole, gesturing for Glitz to follow. They stared out into the void.

Mel let out her breath as Glitz chuckled. 'It's just one of the crew,' he said. 'Routine checks, probably.'

They could see a tether trailing away from the spacesuited figure, presumably anchored to the airlock. 'I can't tell who it is through the helmet,' Mel said.

She felt a flush of embarrassment as the figure revolved towards them, as though they'd been caught peeking. Awkwardly, she turned away from the window.

Glitz gripped her arm, pulling her back. 'Mel!'

She was just in time to see it. The visor of the spacesuit suddenly popped open. Staring out at them, clearly horror-struck, was the face of Frog, the flight engineer.

Mel screamed. She couldn't help it; it felt like she was in a nightmare. Glitz ran to the door, trying to pull it open. When it wouldn't, he began pounding on it, yelling for someone to get to the airlock.

Mel couldn't move. Someone had to realise! Surely any second the figure would be pulled backwards, reeled in, to safety.

But it didn't happen. Frog just floated there, staring at her.

Mel had been on enough spaceships to know what happened next. Space was a dangerous place. Without the protection of an airtight spacesuit, the average human would be finished in minutes. Frog might look as though she was staring at Mel, but she'd surely already lost consciousness. Still, that didn't mean that Frog was doomed – there might still be time to save her life! Someone just had to realise what was happening.

Glitz was still pounding on the door. 'The airlock! Get to the airlock!'

The water on Frog's tongue and eyeballs would be boiling. There would be no blood flowing to her heart or her brain. She would begin to freeze.

Frog's face went pale. Pure white.

Then purple.

Then blue.

Or maybe it didn't. Mel supposed her imagination was colouring it, because she knew she was watching someone die right in front of her. A death that was both incredibly rapid and heart-stoppingly slow, and there was nothing she could do about it.

The only thing she could do now was try to comfort Hope.

She pulled the girl to her chest, shielding her from the horror unfolding outside. Even if they pulled Frog back on board now, they couldn't save her.

But still, nothing happened.

Frog just floated there in space.

Glitz, realising it was already too late, stopped battering the door. That's when they heard the shouts coming from the shuttle bay.

Minutes passed, and then – far, far too late – Frog was dragged away from the porthole.

Mel shut her eyes. She'd felt compelled to keep looking, to bear witness to another human's last, lonely moments, but she was free of that now, and all she wanted to do was erase the image from her mind.

There were sounds of hustle and bustle from the corridor outside, but Mel just kept holding on to Hope.

Eventually, when they'd come to the conclusion that they were being kept in the rec room for good, the door opened.

A grim-looking Pearleye asked them to accompany him to the flight deck.

The rest of the crewmembers were there – whittled down from ten to eight in a matter of hours.

Captain Terle, Pilot Kade, First Officer Demarr and Life System Officer Caleb sat at their own stations. Nash perched on the arm of Demarr's chair; the other three were seated on chairs around the deck.

With a gesture, the captain invited Mel, Glitz and Hope to take seats too.

'Unfortunately, I think we can agree that the death of Frog means the likelihood of Vizhan's death being accidental has decreased considerably,' said the captain.

'Are we sure they couldn't both be accidents?' asked Nash. 'Some component might have perished over the years since the spacesuit was last used.'

Mel felt a surge of friendliness towards the medical officer – if they didn't automatically assume the deaths were murders, it followed that they didn't automatically assume Mel, Glitz and Hope were killers.

The captain shook her head. 'Bastelle and Pearleye have examined the spacesuit. It's their opinion that the damage could only have been caused by sabotage.'

'Well, you can't blame us for this one,' said Glitz. 'We were locked in the whole time!'

Mel shot him a hard stare, but he – perhaps deliberately – didn't look in her direction. She'd been going to make that point too, but maybe in a rather more … *diplomatic* way.

'Frog's suit visor was sabotaged, as were the airlock controls, meaning that we couldn't reach her in time,' said Heide Demarr grimly. 'That could have been done – and probably was done – before the meal.'

'Ah, no,' said Glitz. 'The spacesuits were locked up at that point, and the helmets were still dusty. I noticed that particularly, just before I came to the welcome meal…' He tailed off, and Mel shook her head in disbelief. Of all the ways to protest his innocence, telling people he'd been trying to get at the spacesuits was not the most sensible. But while Glitz's story might be suspicious to the others, it was helpful to Mel – because she felt comfortable taking it at face value. It gave them a *terminus post quem*: the sabotage must have happened *after* Glitz had left the shuttle bay.

She shut her eyes, picturing all the movement back and forth…

'Are we boring you, Mel?' asked Demarr. 'You've been present at a lot of deaths, from what I hear. So this is probably quite run of the mill for you.'

Mel didn't rise to the bait. 'If poison was added to the food or drink, somehow,' she said, eyes still closed, 'it must have happened in either the galley or the crew room. All the supplies from the ship's store were unopened, they couldn't have been dosed beforehand. The only other opportunity would have been to do something to the produce from the hydroponic garden. We can rule out Vizhan, the victim. I can rule out Hope, who helped her gather the fruit and vegetables – I realise that for the rest of you she remains a suspect, but not for me.' She opened her eyes and smiled at the girl. Hope gave a grateful smile in return. 'Hope, was any of the produce out of your sight on the way to the galley? Did anyone pop out of a room and see what you were carrying and examine it?'

Hope shook her head. Mel smiled at her again and closed her eyes for a second time, returning to the scene.

'Now, from the time the produce reached the galley, I was either in the galley too, or in the crew room, setting the table. I would have seen anyone coming down the corridor from the front of the ship. That rules out the captain, Kade, Caleb and Demarr, who were on the flight deck, and Bastelle, Pearleye and – well, and Frog – who were in the engine room.'

'Ahem!' coughed Glitz, loudly.

'Yes, and Glitz, of course.' She opened her eyes and rolled them. 'But anyone from the lower part of the ship could have got into the crew room unseen. So that's Vizhan – and Nash.'

Demarr thumped the desk beside her. 'Nash is utterly incapable—'

The captain cut in. 'Let Mel finish, please. It may prove useful to hear an outsider's perspective on this.'

Demarr rolled her eyes, and Mel hastened to reassure her. 'I'm not accusing Nash of anything – I'm just trying to work this out. It would have been a lot easier for *me* to poison the food than Nash! I'm simply talking about opportunity.

Vizhan, Nash, Hope, Triptolemos and me. Unless the
poison was added at the meal itself, those are the only people
who could have done it. I was sitting next to Vizhan and
I'm sure I would have seen if her food was tampered with.
Other than that, I can't see a way that only *her* food or drink
could have been poisoned. Everything was shared.'

'I would never – never!' began Triptolemos.

Mel, who'd become very fond of the cook during their
time in the galley, said, 'Triptolemos, I really don't think
you'd ever hurt anyone. But I think that about Nash too.' She
hadn't spent a lot of time with the medic, but they had struck
her as kind and caring.

'I don't believe for a second you can rule out everyone
else,' said Demarr. 'You could easily have missed somebody
sneaking past!'

'Sorry,' said Mel with a shrug. 'I just ... don't miss things.'

'You can say that again,' muttered Glitz. He added, more
loudly, 'She's a human camera. Records everything: sight
and sound.' He shrugged. 'What can I say? She's a lot cheaper
than a security system. Hold on – don't you have a security
system? Cameras placed around the ship or—'

'Why would we?' said Bastelle. 'Every crewmember is one
hundred per cent trustworthy.'

'Even *I'm* not one hundred per cent trustworthy,' said Mel.

Bastelle insisted: 'We are all one hundred per cent
trustworthy.'

Livyia raised a hand to silence him, and indicated for Mel
to continue.

'Then we come to what happened to poor Frog.' Mel couldn't help shuddering at the memory of that dead, staring face. 'The spacesuit was still locked up and untouched just before Glitz entered the crew room.' Several mouths opened to disagree with her, but again the captain asked for quiet. 'Hope, Triptolemos and I were already in the crew room, sorting out the food,' Mel went on. 'Frog and Bastelle came in before Glitz, and Glitz and Pearleye entered at the same time. This time, Nash – and Vizhan too, of course – are in the clear; they couldn't have passed the crew room and got to the shuttle bay without me seeing. So, so far, the only people who could have got into the shuttle bay after Glitz left it are Livyia, Kade, Demarr and Caleb. But unfortunately, that's where my knowledge ends. Could anyone have got to the suit after the meal?'

'Absolutely not,' said Bastelle. 'Frog, Pearleye and I were in and out of the shuttle bay right up to the time Frog suited up. One of us would have seen something.'

'Unless one of you –' Glitz dramatically pointed an accusing finger – 'is the killer!'

'Glitz!' Mel found herself adopting the Voice again. He looked sheepish. 'I'm sorry,' said Mel, turning back to Bastelle, 'Glitz may be tactless, but he's right – we do have to put you on the list. So, for murder one, our suspects are Nash, Hope, Triptolemos and me. For the second murder, the suspects are Livyia, Kade, Demarr, Caleb, Pearleye and Bastelle – and we have to add Glitz, as we only have his word that the suit was secure when he looked at it.'

There was silence for a moment. Mel could see everyone processing the information.

'Not a single name is on both lists!' the captain said at last.

Mel nodded. 'I know! Maybe they really were both accidents, however unlikely that seems.'

There was silence again. Then suddenly Demarr spoke. 'There is something you've missed. Or rather, something you hoped *we'd* missed.'

'What?' asked Mel.

'You left the crew room during the meal. You and Glitz. You left just before Vizhan died. Maybe you knew she was going to die and you didn't want to be there for it!'

'No, that wasn't it at all—' Mel began.

But Demarr didn't let her finish. 'Maybe it was a way of creating a distraction, so you could get to the shuttle bay and sabotage the suit and the airlock!'

'We didn't go anywhere near the shuttle bay!' Mel told her – told everyone. 'We went the other way, we were near the rec room when we heard the commotion.'

'You might have gone that way initially,' said Demarr. 'But you could easily have come back while we were distracted by our friend dying in front of us!'

'But we didn't,' Mel insisted.

'Well, unfortunately, none of *us* have perfect recall,' the First Officer said. 'So we only have your word for that. And I'm really not inclined to believe your word.'

'Frog was the one who talked about execution,' said Pearleye. 'That would have given you a grudge against her.'

'Hold on,' said Mel. 'That doesn't even make sense! That didn't happen until *after* Glitz and I were back in the room!'

'But Frog didn't want you to have a shuttle!' put in Caleb. '*That* had been said *before* you left, and proves—'

'All it proves,' sneered Glitz, 'is that Frog was an argumentative little madam.'

Mel shook her head frantically. That was hardly going to make Frog's 'family' give them the benefit of the doubt!

'Not one of us had ever said a cross word to another before you arrived,' put in Pearleye. 'That's why you came, isn't it? To sabotage our mission!'

'But that's ridiculous!' cried Mel. 'Your mission was already sabotaged. We're the ones who *rescued* it!'

She looked to the captain, hoping that Livyia would once again step in to defend her. It didn't happen. Perhaps the time for logic had passed.

All the accusing stares: Pearleye, Caleb, Demarr…

This must be how the women in Salem had felt when their friends and neighbours started to chant: *Witch, witch, witch, witch, witch …*

Mel began to feel very, very scared.

Chapter Thirteen
Body of Proof

On first awakening, Caleb had set the ship's systems to distinguish between day and night. Now, as night approached, the lighting adjusted itself accordingly. But as the light levels dropped, so Mel's fear levels rose.

There had been no more questioning, no more threats – at least, no verbal threats. The captain had stepped in at last to calm everyone down, and had made it clear that the ship's policy was that everyone – Mel, Glitz and Hope included – was innocent until proven guilty. Suspicions, however plausible, did not equal proof in any respect. At the same time, she had decided that the three visitors should be kept under constant supervision.

'Surely it would be in everyone's interests if we just got out of your hair!' Glitz had said.

Demarr had exploded, shouting: 'We're not going to *reward* you with our only shuttle!'

Livyia had had to intervene once more until peace was finally restored.

The five-berth bunk room was for the male crew: Kade, Caleb, Bastelle, Triptolemos and Pearleye. The three-berth bunk room housed the female crew – that would have been Demarr, Frog and Vizhan. Livyia, as captain, slept in the one-person quarters adjoining the flight deck, where she was permanently on call overnight. Nash had their own quarters off the medical centre; as ship's medic they too were constantly on call.

With Demarr's agreement, Nash was going to move – temporarily – into the female quarters, and Mel and the others would spend the night in Nash's room. Assigning rooms the other way round would have made more sense from a practical point of view, but Demarr became so irate at the thought of any of the newcomers sleeping in Frog or Vizhan's spots that she actually yelled at the captain for suggesting it.

Instead, they ended up piling blankets on the floor of the tiny room for Glitz and Mel, while Hope took the medic's bed.

'Wake up your bouffant beau,' Glitz said after the three of them were alone. 'He needs to get us access to that shuttle before we all get And-Then-There-Were-None-ed.'

Mel sighed. 'He's not my "beau" and he's already said he can't do that. We have to be physically inducted into the system, apparently.'

'Hmmm.' Glitz looked thoughtful. 'That would be Bastelle's bailiwick. Anyone got any blackmailable information on the gentleman?'

'No, and I imagine he wouldn't do it without the captain's say-so whatever the circumstances. Anyway, we can't just leave, not like this.'

'I disagree with you, Melanie. We can leave like this and we should leave like this. And given the opportunity, I most certainly will leave like this. It would pain me very much to terminate our mutually beneficial working partnership, but ...'

'No!' cried Hope, looking as though she was going to burst into tears. 'You can't do that! You can't!'

'He won't,' Mel said, with more certainty than she felt. 'If we leave, we all leave together.'

'Me too?' asked Hope. Like a scared child, she added, 'You promise you won't leave me behind?'

'Of course we won't,' said Mel. 'You're welcome on the *Nosferatu II*. And Glitz agrees.'

She shot a 'be nice' look at him, but to Glitz's credit he answered immediately.

'Course you're welcome, junior! And I'm not even going to charge you rent!'

To Mel's relief, the girl smiled at that. She was already getting the hang of Glitz and his ways. 'I'll pay you back by helping in your garden. I'd really like to try making plants.'

'*Growing* plants,' Mel corrected automatically. 'But I'm sorry, Hope, we don't have a garden. Most spaceships don't,

I'm afraid.' She couldn't bear to see the disappointment on Hope's face, though, and added, 'But I'm sure we could find a way! Oh, come on –' that was to Glitz, who looked extremely doubtful – 'we could grow our own carrots! Or even make our own jam!'

'If you feel the desire to be a botanical boffin, who am I to stand in your way?' said Glitz. 'But the flaw in your plan – the *Calliphora vomitoria* in the ointment, so to speak – is your aforementioned reluctance to liberate the aforesaid shuttlecraft.'

Mel tried to explain her reasoning. She knew – and Glitz and Hope presumably knew too – that none of them were the murderer. Which meant that, if there really was a killer, it was one of the *Kazemi*'s crew.

'So if we take their only remaining shuttle,' Mel said, 'and the murders continue – there's no escape for any of them. We don't know the murderer's motive, and there are 75 million people on board – 75 million lives at stake! What happens to them if all of Crew D gets wiped out?' She shrugged. 'But the point is moot. As it stands, we *can't* leave.'

They all sat in thought for a few moments.

Then Mel said in exasperation, 'If we can't get off the ship, our only hope is to find the killer! Except I've already worked out that it can't be any of us. How can there be murders when there's no murderer?'

'If I were the captain,' said Glitz, 'I'd be back in the deep freeze before you could say Jack Robinson. Hand over to some other crew.'

'Livyia won't do that,' said Mel. 'She thinks it's her responsibility to sort this out.'

'And what if the murders continued anyway?' said Hope.

A slight intake of breath from Glitz. 'You, junior, have just hit on something that me and my girl Mel here have overlooked until now. We've been rather hasty in limiting the suspects to eleven. If we take the pool of suspects as –' he started counting on his fingers – 'eleven plus 75 million plus – how many crews?'

'Ten, including Crew D,' said Mel. 'But we know that Crew C are all d—'

'No, we don't,' Glitz cut over her. 'One or two could have escaped from the platform and gone mad. They could've been hiding in the ducting for the last however-many years! So that's another eighty, perhaps eighty-one. I'm just pointing out that if you assume a population of seventy-five million and ninety-two, the odds of the killer being one of us three have lengthened considerably.'

Mel thought about it. That did actually make sense. 'We should speak to Livyia,' she said at last. 'She could arrange a search. Maybe Bastelle can look on the ship's system. He might be able to find out if there have been any unauthorised awakenings or unminiaturisations. And he might be able to identify potential hiding places too.' She let out a breath. 'It'd be such a relief if you're right. I mean, Crew D think of each other as family.'

'Family's not all that,' said Glitz. 'Statistically speaking, almost fifty per cent of homicides are committed by a family member. Actually, on Salostopus, almost fifty per cent of that fifty per cent of family murders were committed by my half-cousin Oomalon Glitz. A very painful subject,' he added. 'I'd appreciate it if we could just leave it there.'

'Um ... OK,' said Mel, who was fine not hearing the details. 'But the crewmembers insist there's never been a cross word between any of them.'

'Apart from all the cross words we've heard today,' Glitz said.

Mel sighed. 'Well, obviously it's a slight exaggeration. I mean, I had the occasional spat with my mum, but—' She broke off at the sound of a sob. 'Hope! Oh, Hope, I'm so sorry. I wasn't thinking.'

The girl had pulled out the tiny embroidery of the word HOPE – the only thing she'd taken with her from the *Seraphine* – and was hugging it to her.

'I wish you'd been able to know your parents,' Mel told the girl. 'But you will find a family, some day. Family isn't just blood, you know. No –' she went on as Glitz opened his mouth to speak – 'This is not the time to mention how much blood your family spilled or anything like that, thank you very much.' She leaned over and gave Hope a hug. 'Why don't you lie down now and try to have a sleep.'

'I thought you wanted us to keep watch all night?' said Hope.

Mel shook her head. 'Glitz and I can do that. You rest.'

'OK.'

'You can join her, Mel,' said Glitz. 'I'll take the first shift.'

Mel smiled gratefully. Even her usually boundless energy had limits, and the emotion of the day had worn her out. 'Let's just go over it all again first,' she said, 'and then a rest would be wonderful! Thank you.' She marshalled her thoughts. 'The flight deck overnight rota has Kade on duty from ten till one, Caleb from one till four, and Demarr from four till seven. So those three will be alone at certain times, but the captain sleeps pretty much on the flight deck and will hear if anything happens.'

'Is there really that much to do overnight?' asked Glitz.

Mel shrugged. 'I think it's just that they've all got a really strong work ethic. No one else should be on their own overnight, except for Nash during Demarr's shift on the flight deck. But as Bastelle, Triptolemos and Pearleye have all decided to take a shift overnight to watch over the sleeping quarters – meaning us – no one can get to Nash unseen. So there'll be a minimum of two people awake and alert at all times on the ship, as well as us.'

There was a glass panel in the door of the room Mel and Glitz were in, which looked onto the medical centre (although 'medical centre' was rather a grand name for what it was). The centre opened onto the side passage that led to first the female and then the male bunk rooms: when its door was open, everyone's comings and goings could be seen.

Mel and Glitz planned to each take a turn on watch overnight. They were, of course, locked in – and were aware that even if they did see anything, Crew D would be unlikely to take their word for it.

Even so, for Mel, this came under the heading of 'better safe than sorry'.

With a command of 'Wake up!' Barry was once more summoned from his cube like the genie from *Aladdin* – at least each sentry would have some company overnight. He and Glitz settled down on watch, and Mel retired to get some rest.

Lying on her not-very-comfortable blanket bed, Mel shut her eyes and tried to quiet her brain. She couldn't stop replaying the day in her mind: everything that had led up to each murder, and beyond. If only she'd been in the crew room when Vizhan died – she couldn't have saved her, she knew that, but perhaps she would have seen something, a person's expression for instance, that could have given them a clue …

Had she seen *anything* strange, anything at all, since Crew D awoke?

After some thought, only two things came to mind: the moment in the galley where Triptolemos had suddenly seemed to freeze, and Frog's irritation with Demarr at the dinner table. There had been a few other moments of annoyance or argument, but they all had external causes – such as if they should let Mel and Glitz have the shuttle, for instance, or Vizhan and Nash's clash over chemicals. Small as they were, it was those two incidents alone that stood out. Mel mulled them over and over, and finally realised the cause.

Someone had poisoned the carrot cocktail!

Yes! There was someone hiding in the walls of the ship, who only came out at night. They had to make sure none of the humans developed night vision because then they might see them creeping around in the dark, and carrots were well known for boosting eyesight! So this nocturnal infiltrator had formed an army of sentient tomatoes to destroy the carrots, which was even now swarming through the ship singing ABBA songs ...

... and Mel woke up as Glitz shook her shoulder. 'Wakey-wakey, sunbeam,' he whispered. 'Three of the clock and all's well. Nothing to report. Caleb went past on his way to the flight deck, that was a couple of hours ago, and a minute or two later Kade came back. I am, however, considering admitting I am the killer and throwing myself on the captain's mercy if I have to hear any more squirrel jokes.'

Mel sat up, only semi-awake and still half on alert for the tomato army stomping across the floor wielding cleavers and singing 'Chiquitita'. For a moment she thought she was still dreaming, because top pop pin-up Barry Day was waving at her ...

Then it all came rushing back. She returned his wave. 'OK, you get some sleep now,' she said to Glitz, and went to sit next to the AI.

'Hey Mel,' he whispered. 'Where does Squixy wash her clothes?'

'Um ... I don't know.'

'At the laun-*drey*-mat!'

* * *

What a strange situation this was, thought Mel.

Her teenage crush belonged to years ago, another time and another place, and probably, if she thought about it, another person. It hadn't been serious, just schoolgirl stuff. She wasn't the sort of person who'd cried when Dutch Elm Disease split up; she didn't hang on Barry's every word or refuse to leave the house on Saturday mornings if it meant missing *Spaceship Saturday*. Yes, she'd thought he was cute – and yes, she'd had the odd daydream of the two of them, lying on a blanket out by the lake at Tilbrook Park, watching the stars (Barry pointing out Orion or the Seven Sisters... Maybe there'd be a meteor shower if they were really lucky...). But if she was honest, she was more interested in the astronomy aspect of that situation than the romantic one. Romance, for Mel, was travel, adventure, excitement – those were the things that stirred her heart.

And she'd been granted those things, in abundance.

But there was still something pleasant about sitting quietly in the dark with Barry Day whispering in her ear, even if he was only whispering squirrel jokes.

'Hey Mel, what does Squixy pull at Christmas?'

'Oh, hold on, I can get this ... A nut-cracker!'

'Well done, lass!'

Mel laughed – quietly. She glanced over at her sleeping friends. Hope had her mother's embroidery on the pillow beside her, one hand resting on it: a sweet if melancholy pose. Glitz, neither sweet nor melancholy, was lying flat on his back and snoring loudly. Both sights made her smile.

In between the jokes, Mel and Barry discussed Glitz's theories and, to Mel's astonishment, the AI was able to confirm that there were various places on the ship – tunnels, ducting, service hatches – from which someone could access the main body of the ship, but remain hidden most of the time. ('Hey Mel, what's a nuthatch?' 'Isn't it a bird, Barry?' 'No – it's how Squixy accesses the ship's ducting!') But he soon squashed her hopes of finding a hidden murderer. The ship's systems had detected no movement for years until Mel and co came on board.

Even without carrots, Mel's eyes had quickly got used to the gloom. After an hour or so, she saw Demarr pass down the side passage towards the main corridor. A few minutes later Caleb went by in the opposite direction, his shift on the flight deck complete. The ship was so silent that she even heard him say, 'Night, Bastelle,' as he headed for his bed.

When a light went on in the medical centre, perhaps fifteen minutes later, Mel had to shut her eyes for a moment from the unexpected glare.

When she opened them again, she could see the medical officer, TC Nash, rummaging through a cabinet.

Mel didn't draw attention to herself, and moved to sit at an angle where she could see out without being seen. She'd liked Nash from the few interactions they'd had, but surely this was suspicious behaviour? It was the middle of the night!

She watched as Nash climbed on a chair to examine the contents of a high shelf – and then climbed back down, a small bottle in hand. Lotion? Poison? Acid?

Nash put the bottle in their pocket. It looked as though they were going to leave – and then at the last moment, they turned towards the sleeping quarters where Mel and Barry sat. Mel saw them frown – and then approach. Nash tapped on the door, very, very quietly, then unlocked it and, still being very, very quiet, pushed it open.

Mel, standing, backed away. Nash held up their hands. 'Sorry, did I frighten you?' they whispered. 'I caught a glimpse of Barry through the window.'

They beckoned to her, and Mel, slightly warily, stepped out. 'Barry, wait there,' she said. If she was being lured to her doom, she needed him to barricade the door and protect Hope and Glitz.

'I'm sorry if I disturbed you,' Nash said. 'I woke up when Demarr went for her shift. Then something occurred to me, and I couldn't get it out of my head, so I came to check.' They sat down, and gestured for Mel to sit beside them. 'There aren't many medications in here; having A-one health's part of the selection process, of course. My main role is to deal with injuries, or any complications in coming out of suspended animation. But I do have chemicals …' They held up the bottle Mel had seen them take earlier. 'Crew C's medic would usually have done an audit of all substances before swap-over, but I only have their daily notes. Going by those, there are two fewer pills than there should be. But the medic might have dispensed them and not had a chance to record it.'

'Who would have had access to the pills?' Mel asked.

'Everyone.' Nash let out an irritated breath. 'But every member of the crew is utterly trustworthy. I'd bet my life on that.'

Mel didn't say that they might be called upon to do so.

Nash carried on. 'I just want this nightmare to be over. It's affecting everyone. Frog, Demarr – they never used to be like that.'

It was an awkward topic to broach, but Mel said, as lightly as she could, 'Frog and Demarr – there seemed to be a little … rivalry going on?'

Nash looked embarrassed. 'As I said, they weren't like this on previous awakenings. Relationships within crews … well, they're not forbidden, as such, but part of the selection process was making sure that things like that … wouldn't happen. Our sole responsibility – our sole *purpose* – is the future of our people.'

That was admirable, of course, but … 'You don't get to have a life of your own at all?'

'What could be more fulfilling than the knowledge that you're preserving your whole civilisation?'

Mel thought back to Livyia's toast at the welcome meal, before tragedy intervened. 'The captain said, "Our journey is long, and we who are privileged to have been chosen as guardians of our people know that we will not live to see our destination." Is that true? You'll die before you reach the end?'

'Oh yes.' Nash gave the saddest of smiles. 'Back home – Earth, you know – scientists discovered that a strange force was exerting itself on the planet. They were worried it might actually pull the planet out of orbit, which would kill every living thing immediately, of course. But they found a way to protect us – for a while. We already had teams for deep space exploration, and we'd started to use suspended animation and miniaturisation for people in those fields. It took months that we didn't really have, but they worked on the technology, and began to recruit the crews. We got off the planet just in time. Our instruments showed that soon after we set off, the Earth – the entire *constellation*! – had just … gone. Completely destroyed.'

Mel hadn't realised quite how much of a boon time travel was. It didn't matter where she went in the TARDIS – she knew her home would always be waiting for her. She resolved to investigate as soon as she got back to the *Nosferatu II*. Surely there must be such a thing as a time taxi? Not that she had any intention of going back to Earth in the foreseeable future; it would just be comforting to know that she *could*, if she wanted to …

'So where are you heading?' she asked Nash. 'I assume you've got a destination in mind.'

'The ship is programmed to find a planet as similar to the Earth as possible. We hadn't been in space that long before it found one. It's perfect. Practically identical to Earth – it could be its twin! Even the constellation it's in is almost indistinguishable from ours! But it's a long, long way away. We all knew there was a chance we wouldn't see the end of the voyage, and that just confirmed it as a certainty.

We'll keep cycling through the crews as long as possible; we can even continue to operate with reduced numbers. But we have the final crew – Crew J – who won't be awakened until the last of Crews A to I are gone. They will bring the ship home. The *new* home.'

The new home that Mel was practically certain was called Ravolox.

But Ravolox was no paradise, no home-from-home for the escapees from Earth, Mel knew that. Why were they giving their lives for it, when there were thousands of other suitable planets they could reach much, much sooner?

'We don't deviate from the course,' Nash said, when Mel asked the question.

'Why not?'

But Nash didn't seem to be able to give an answer, didn't even seem to really understand the question. They just kept saying, 'We don't deviate from the course.'

Mel couldn't face the one-sided argument, and cast around for a change of subject. 'Oh!' she said. 'Fingerprints!'

'What?'

'I suppose it's so low tech, all Sherlock Holmes with a magnifying glass, that I never even thought of it before. There might be fingerprints on the spacesuit store – there might be fingerprints on that bottle! Do you have any powder? And an insufflator?'

'I could probably find powder of some sort,' said Nash. 'And I expect there's something we can use with it. Oh Mel, do you really think we could find out who's behind this?'

'Yes, I do! The crew's fingerprints must be on the system somewhere – Barry?' She beckoned for the AI to join them. 'Can you access the ship's database and find finger-print records?'

'Course I can, lass! Hey, lasses – why does Squixy love her job?'

'Could we do jokes afterwards please, Barry, we're a bit busy—'

'Because it pays peanuts!'

Nash had screwed up their face, frowning.

'I know,' said Mel. 'That's a *terrible* joke.'

'It's not that.' They reached into their pocket and drew out a piece of paper. 'I found this on the floor under Frog's bed – what used to be Frog's bed. I was going to ask people in the morning if they had any idea what it was about, but that's why I knocked on the door when I saw Barry – I thought he might be able to tell me what it means, because it mentions Squixy. But I realise now, it's a joke, just like that one.'

They handed Mel the paper, and she read it. '"How does Squixy show her appreciation? With a round of a-paws." You found this under Frog's bed? That doesn't make any sense!'

Nash suddenly put a finger to their lips. 'Mel … did you hear something?' they whispered.

Mel shook her head. But then she *did* hear something, a hissing noise—

And that was the last thing she knew for some hours.

Chapter Fourteen

Death in Paradise

'Mel. Melanie! Come on, stir yourself, will you?'

'Go away, it's Saturday,' Mel muttered.

'Melanie!'

Finally, she managed to pull herself more or less awake. She was on a blanket bed in the room off the medical bay, and Glitz was standing over her. He didn't look happy. 'What's wrong?' she asked, as she attempted to sit up.

'Oh, hardly anything. Very little reason to be concerned that we're stuck here until we can get our hands on that shuttle! Only that this morning you, Nash and Bastelle were discovered unconscious, and Demarr is missing.'

'Oh no!' She really was awake now.

'And that's not the worst of it.'

Mel was scared now. 'What?'

Glitz sighed. 'Might be better if you see that bit for yourself.' He offered her a hand up, and she took it.

185

'I remember sitting talking to Nash ...' she said. 'Then ... No. I'm not sure what happened. Hold on, though, where's Barry? He must have seen everything.'

'Your synthetic friend is missing. And no, before you ask, that is not the "worst of it" to which I earlier made reference.'

They reached the corridor, and Glitz guided her towards the hydroponic garden. 'This is where they're searching now,' he said, as they stepped inside.

'Sorry, crew only. We have to be careful, as I'm sure you understand. I suggest you wait in the rec room for now – someone will come and tell you if there's any news.'

Mel stared in astonishment. What on earth ...?

'See what I mean?' Glitz murmured.

'Hope!' said Mel. 'What's happened to you?' How could the person talking to them so officiously be *Hope*?

'Nothing's "happened to me", Mel,' Hope said. 'I'm afraid you just have to accept that the safety of this ship and of Crew D is of more importance right now than your feelings.'

'Over here!' The shout came from further into the garden – Mel thought the voice was Caleb's.

'Stay there,' Hope ordered brusquely and hurried off.

Mel and Glitz looked at each other, clearly in unspoken agreement.

Hope was still limping, so it wasn't particularly hard to keep up with her. They stumbled onto a sombre scene: lying flat on a bed of leaves, her arms crossed and vines weaved into her long blonde hair, was Heide Demarr. A knife stuck out of her chest.

'Oh no,' breathed Mel.

Nash was kneeling beside the body. 'Don't touch anything!' they ordered.

'I thought Nash was unconscious too?' Mel said to Glitz.

'They were. You were the last to wake up.'

Nash pulled on surgical gloves and removed the knife gingerly. 'All right,' they said, 'you can move her now. And we'll test this for fingerprints.' They actually smiled at Mel. 'Mel's idea.'

Mel attempted to smile back. She was so confused! But at least no one was accusing her of killing Demarr. Whatever had happened to her last night, at least it had given her an alibi ...

Caleb and Kade picked up Demarr's body and carried her away, presumably to the engineering level where Vizhan and Frog had previously been taken.

'This has been another terrible shock,' Livyia said to those remaining. 'But we must carry on. Please return to your normal work. Mel and Glitz – if you would kindly wait in the rec room for now.'

'What about Hope?' Mel asked. 'She should stay with us!'

'Demarr's death means we have a suboptimal quota for effective ship management,' replied the captain. 'Under those circumstances, Hope has agreed to assist us.'

'But ... Hope doesn't know anything about manning a spacecraft!'

'You forget,' said Hope, 'I have lived my entire life on a spaceship.'

'Yes, but …'

Glitz took hold of Mel's arm. 'There's no point,' he said. 'Come on, let's go to the rec room. We can have a game of gin rummy.'

Glitz slammed down his hand of cards. 'You're cheating.'

'I am not!' Mel was indignant.

'You must be!' insisted Glitz. 'We've gone through every card game I know, and you've won all of them!'

'I am *not* cheating!'

'But *I am*!'

'What?'

Glitz huffed in annoyance. 'I have been cheating every single time, and you're still winning!' He narrowed his eyes. 'That amazing memory of yours … You're counting cards!'

'Of course I'm not! And you must know I'd never cheat!'

'Hmm.' Glitz gathered in all the cards and shuffled the deck. 'We'll try again.'

He dealt the cards and, very slowly and deliberately, studied every move Mel made. 'You are! You're counting cards!'

'I'm not!' Mel said again.

'There's no way you would've played that Jack if you hadn't known where all the diamonds were.'

'But of course I knew where all the diamonds were!'

'Because you're counting cards!'

'I am not counting cards! I just remember where every card is in the deck!'

There was silence for a few moments, then Glitz said, oh so lightly, 'That, Melanie, is counting cards,' and put his head in his hands.

'Oh,' said Mel. 'I didn't know that.'

'How could you not know that?' he said, his voice muffled. 'Has someone blanked out bits of your memory?'

'No! It's just never come up before!'

'Ah,' said Glitz, with a 'gotcha!' intonation, 'but if someone blanked out bits of your memory, how would you know?'

'I'd just ... know,' said Mel.

Still hiding his face, Glitz shook his head.

The silence continued.

'I'm sorry?' Mel tried, when Glitz didn't move again.

At last he raised his head, and she braced herself for his annoyance. But instead, his face split into a huge grin. 'Mel,' he said. 'What a future we have ahead of us. Every space casino in the twelve galaxies is ours for the taking!'

'Absolutely not,' said Mel. 'And I'm not playing cards with you anymore, either.'

There was a sound that might have been a muffled snort of laughter from Kade. Various crewmembers had been in and out of the rec room over the course of the morning. At first, Mel had been circumspect in her conversations with Glitz, but soon reasoned she had nothing to hide. She might even convert one of their guards ...

Now she returned to the thing that had occupied her for most of the morning. Once the fuss had died down, she'd remembered the last few moments with Nash before they'd both been rendered unconscious somehow. 'If we could just trace the handwriting on that note!' she said.

'Can't you remember what it looked like?' asked Glitz.

'Yes – but I don't imagine the crew will all submit handwriting samples for me to compare it to. And without the note as evidence, no one would believe me if I *did* work out who wrote it.'

'I wouldn't be averse to learning who our homicidal shipmate is,' said Glitz. 'I'm not unused to needing eyes in the back of my head, but it can get wearying over time.'

Mel sighed. 'If I'd been thinking clearly last night, I'd have realised what that note was for. As soon as I said "paws" …'

'Which sounds the same as *pause,* and shut down Barry the Bionic Boy. You do realise that the most likely person to have done that is Nash? They show you the note, knock out you and Pearleye, do the dreadful deed and then pretend to have been comatose all along!'

'I know,' said Mel. 'But I liked them. And they seemed genuine to me. If only we could find Barry's cube! He or Squixy might have seen something before the AI was switched off. But a thing that small could be anywhere. Oh well. Maybe we'll learn something from fingerprints.'

'First handwriting, now fingerprints? We're going to have to call you Mel Marple,' said Glitz.

It was Nash who brought them some food at lunchtime. 'I know it can't have been either of you who killed Demarr,' they said. 'You were with me –' that was to Mel – 'when we were rendered unconscious, and Glitz was asleep. But the captain has asked me to take your fingerprints anyway.'

'I suppose at least that'll rule us out,' said Mel.

Glitz looked horrified. 'One does not voluntarily share one's details with law enforcement, my girl!'

'I don't imagine we've got a lot of choice.' Mel looked at Nash. 'Do we?'

'Sorry,' they said.

'Have you actually checked for fingerprints on the knife?' Mel asked, as she rolled her fingertips on a glass slide.

Nash nodded. 'Yes. There are a few clear prints – none of which are from any member of the crew.'

'But what about *other* crews? Barry could be wrong. What if there really is someone hiding on the ship?'

'I don't know. I'll ask the captain. Don't worry. You'll be out of here soon, I'm sure.'

Glitz offered Mel a Galactasnax bar as Nash left the room.

'We've just been handed lunch!' Mel pointed out.

'And I for one am *totally* certain it's not been poisoned,' said Glitz.

Mel accepted the Galactasnax bar.

Nash was right. It wasn't long before Mel and Glitz were out of the rec room. The announcement 'Kade, please escort Mel and Glitz to the flight deck,' came through the intercom, and the pilot did as bidden.

All of Crew D – and Hope – were waiting for them on the flight deck.

For Mel, it brought back memories of facing the court when the Doctor had been put on trial for his life. But instead of being a witness, she was now the defendant.

The captain stood up. 'Mel, Glitz, thank you for joining us.'

'We didn't exactly have a choice,' muttered Glitz.

'Thank you also for your cooperation,' Livyia continued. 'Even if it does seem that you have been – as an old Earth saying has it – "hoist with your own petard".'

'What do you mean?' asked Mel.

'That you've been blown off the ground by your own explosive device,' Glitz hissed out of the side of his mouth.

'I understand the poetic justice! I meant, why is she saying it?'

Livyia cleared her throat. 'I'm referring to your suggestion to Nash that the killer may have left fingerprints when carrying out the previous crimes – and then you leave your own fingerprints on a murder weapon. It's been claimed you have a remarkable memory, so I'm assuming this wasn't forgetfulness – just overconfidence, perhaps?'

'What?' Mel swapped glances with Glitz, who looked equally alarmed. 'Are you saying that my fingerprints were on the knife?'

'They were, yes.'

'Oh!' Mel felt a rush of relief. 'But they would be, if the knife was from the kitchen. I spent hours in there cutting things up for the welcome meal – you know that!'

'We've considered that,' said the captain. 'But Triptolemos assures us—'

The cook jumped in to complete the sentence. 'In my kitchen, every knife is washed so clean, it is as though it had never been used at all!'

'Well, one must have been missed,' said Mel. 'That's the only explanation.'

'But Glitz didn't cut up things in the galley.' Hope joined in the discussion. 'I was there the whole time, and he didn't come in once.'

'I ... never said he did,' said Mel, confused.

'But you see, his fingerprints were on the knife too,' said the captain. 'Both your fingerprints ... and no one else's.'

Mel's head was spinning. The evidence had been faked in some way, obviously, but how? And how would she prove it to the increasingly hostile crew?

Then the solution hit her.

'Could I see the knife, please?'

There were grumbles at that, but Livyia overruled the dissenters. 'But I will ask you not to touch it,' she said, as Nash produced the weapon.

Mel gave a huge sigh of relief when she saw the knife. 'You recognise it, don't you, Glitz?' she said. 'That's the knife I got from the galley – you used the blade to prise open the entrance to the awakening room, remember?' She turned back to the captain. 'That's why it's got both our fingerprints on it! And it wasn't used to prepare food, so it didn't get washed up with the rest of the cutlery.'

'And furthermore,' Glitz put in, 'if we hadn't used it, you and your bunch of dilettante detectives here would still be snoring away in cold storage. Don't forget you owe us.'

There was some grumbling and mumbling from the crew. 'It is a plausible explanation,' said Livyia.

'Hope was there when I took the knife into the hydroponic garden,' said Mel. 'Hope? You remember, don't you?'

The girl nodded. Whatever had caused her change in behaviour, at least she hadn't turned against them.

Livyia asked Mel and Glitz to return to the rec room, sending Caleb to accompany them.

Mel reached the door and turned back. It was probably a mistake to ask, but … 'Hope,' she said. 'You do still want to come with us, don't you? Back to our ship?'

Hope looked almost pityingly at Mel. 'My duty is with the *Kazemi*,' she said. 'Their mission is important.'

'More important than having your own little garden?'

'More important than any of our *lives*.'

Chapter Fifteen

Perception

'I've narrowed down the possibilities,' Glitz said a short time later, back in the rec room. 'Doppelganger or voodoo.'

'Hope, you mean?' Mel lowered her voice. Caleb was at the Space Invaders cabinet and didn't seem to be paying any attention, but she didn't want to give the crew ammunition against any of them, Hope included. 'She's been through a lot, remember. Her moods have been up and down even since we arrived here.'

'That was not a person either up *or* down,' said Glitz. 'That was a person with a top to tail personality change. Doppelganger! Voodoo! Zombie! Hypnosis!'

'I suppose it's not impossible that she's been hypnotised – but by who? And why?'

'The why's obvious enough. To kill people!'

Mel shook her head.

'Hope has not been hypnotised to kill people, that's ridiculous.'

'Good point,' said Glitz. 'On further consideration, I am in agreement with you. She wouldn't need to be hypnotised.'

'That's not what I—'

'She comes from a "family" as dysfunctional as the Caesars – or the Borgias – or the Slitheen! Might not take much to push her over the edge, hence what we're seeing now: Jack the Ripper Junior.'

'That doesn't feel right at all,' said Mel. 'And anyway, it's impossible. Literally impossible, in the case of Frog – Hope didn't have the opportunity to get at either the spacesuit or the airlock, and she most definitely doesn't have the skills needed to sabotage them.'

'She could have got the poison from the medic's room, though. She was in there before the meal, remember? Getting her leg looked at.'

'Her leg – that's just the point,' said Mel. 'The pills were on a high shelf. She couldn't have climbed up to get them. No, whatever's going on with Hope, we can cross her off the list of suspects.'

With cards verboten, Glitz dug through the games and brought out Milky Way Monopoly. He half-heartedly set up the board. Neither was exactly enthusiastic about it, and they hardly noticed how frequently the game paused while one or the other of them drifted off into thought.

Mel had just drawn a card telling her to 'Go to Desperus. Go directly to Desperus. Do not pass GO, do not collect 200 nargs', when Kade came in; he announced that he fancied another break, so Caleb could go and make himself useful for a change.

Out of all of their 'guards', Kade was easily the friendliest. 'Mind if I join?' he asked. 'Haven't played that since I was a kid!'

'Yes, of course,' said Mel. Glitz rolled his eyes at that, but she would have felt rude saying no. And anyway, having friendly relations with any of the crew could only be a good thing in their current circumstances.

Kade pulled up a chair between them, and reached for the pile of narg notes in front of him.

'Mine, I *think* you'll find,' said Glitz grimly, reclaiming them, as Mel started to dish out Kade's starter's share from the bank. Then she stopped, frozen, her hand in midair.

'Glitz to Melanie, Glitz to Melanie, come in, Melanie!'

'Don't distract me!'

She closed her eyes. Had she stumbled on something at last? 'Can you remember where everyone was sitting at the welcome meal?' she said.

'You mean you can't?' said Glitz, sounding surprised.

'Just humour me. Please.'

'All right, all right. Clockwise from the head ... Livyia. My side of the table: this gentleman here, then Hope, me, Pearleye, Frog, and ...'

'Nash,' Kade put in. 'Then Demarr at the foot of the table.'

'Then Caleb, Barry, Vizhan, you, Bastelle — and Triptolemos on Livyia's left.'

Kade agreed. 'He usually sits there, so he's closest to the door. That just makes it easier if he's bringing in food from the galley.'

Mel opened her eyes and laid out a row of notes from the ones in her hand: 1 narg, 5 narg, 10 narg, 20 narg, 50 narg. 'This is my side of the table at the welcome meal,' she said, then pointed to each different note in turn: 'Trip, Bastelle, me, Vizhan, Caleb.'

'You've forgotten Barry,' Glitz said.

She shook his head. 'No, I haven't.' She then laid out another identical row behind it. 'And these are our plates. So, Caleb is the 50 narg note and he eats off the 50 narg plate.'

'Don't I get to be a note?' asked Glitz. 'I'd say the 500 narg has my name on it ...'

'We only need this side,' said Mel. She took her playing piece – the bow-tie-wearing Garm – and put it in between the first 20 and 50 narg notes, moving all those to the left of it along one place. Now the 50 narg note was still in front of the other 50 narg note – but the Garm faced the second 20 narg note, the first 20 narg note faced the second 10 narg note, and so on down the line until the first 1 narg note faced nothing at all.

'Well, this has been fun,' said Glitz with a yawn. 'I thought I was already bored, but little did I know a game of "Pass the narg" was going to come along. Truly I am having the time of my life.'

'Look,' said Mel. She indicated the silver Garm. 'This is Barry. When he appeared, Vizhan moved along – but she didn't move her plate. They were all the same, they were all untouched, why would she?'

'Because "Barry" is a semi-solid artificial intelligence who doesn't need to eat?' Glitz suggested.

'Well, yes – but she might not have thought of that in the moment. Or perhaps she was worried about seeming rude? We'll never know. But can't you see? If Barry had Vizhan's plate, and we all moved along one ...'

'Stone the corvids!' cried Glitz. 'Are you sure?'

'I think so. Vizhan ate from what should have been *my* plate. She wasn't the intended victim – I was!'

Mel's deduction appeared to have affected Glitz deeply. 'You were the intended victim ...' he kept muttering, looking concerned – even distressed.

'It's all right!' said Mel comfortingly. 'I wasn't hurt – and now we know about it, I'll be even more careful than I've been already.'

'Good for you!' said Glitz, not looking comforted at all by her words. 'But you seem to have overlooked a particularly salient point, which is that they might be targeting me too!'

'Oh,' said Mel.

'Do you not realise, Melanie, that *I* was looking at that spacesuit before the meal! Maybe someone thought I was going to use it!'

'That's a bit of a stretch ...' Mel began.

He held up a hand to stop her. 'And young Hope has been spending a lot of time in the hydroponic garden. Maybe someone mistook Demarr for her! Oh, it's a classic case. Outsiders unwelcome! How many holovids and digibooks have been made on such a theme ...'

Mel found her own deduction – that she, rather than Vizhan, had been targeted – to be convincing. Glitz's theorising, on the other hand, didn't ring quite as true. 'I think you'd have to be a *really* inefficient murderer to kill the wrong person on three separate occasions,' she pointed out.

'None of us would have killed Frog or Demarr, though,' said Kade, who'd been listening intently. 'Of course, I can't imagine any of us trying to kill any of you either – but to kill a fellow crewmember? It's unthinkable. Literally. Such a thought would never enter our heads under any circumstances.'

'Wait! That gives me an idea,' said Mel. 'Let me think ...'

Glitz held out a hand for Kade to shake. 'Congratulations,' he said. 'Welcome to the ranks of the honorary Watsons, forever doomed to utter innocuous phrases that trigger the genius of others. Pray tell, what was this significant sentence, Melanie Marple?'

'About thoughts entering heads. And there was also what you said, Glitz, when we were playing cards. You asked if someone had blanked out bits of my memory. And you mentioned hypnotism earlier too! I think that's what's been happening! The murderer commits the murder, then just ... doesn't remember it.'

'Hmmm.' Glitz looked at Kade. 'How plausible does that sound to you?'

The pilot shrugged his shoulders. 'Not very, I'm afraid.'

'Shame. It's a beautiful excuse. "Not guilty, your honour, by reason of being hypnotised."'

Mel was still working it out. 'Both Vizhan's and Frog's murders were ... I suppose you'd call it "delayed action" deaths. The food was poisoned, the spacesuit was sabotaged, but the victims didn't die until later.'

'But Demarr was stabbed,' said Kade.

'You're right,' said Mel. 'But it was a murder with a lot of preparations. Leaving that note, gassing potential witnesses, stealing the knife with our fingerprints on. These are all planned murders, none of them happen in the heat of the moment. That points to serious darkness inside someone here. How could they hide that darkness from the people who know them best? I don't think they could. I think that – other than at certain points, when they were actively involved in organising or committing the crime – the murderer *didn't know* they were the murderer. They were just a puppet.'

'I *knew* that squirrel was suspect!' cried Glitz.

'That's not what I meant,' said Mel. 'All along, we've known that the most likely person to have poisoned the food is Triptolemos.'

'Absolutely not—' began Kade.

Mel was sympathetic, but stopped him anyway. 'This is just theorising. But there's something I haven't told anyone about. There was a moment, in the kitchen. When we were preparing the welcome meal. Triptolemos sort of ... froze.'

'Froze?'

'It was only a few moments, but his face went blank. At the time, I wondered if he was upset with me. But now ... was that the exact moment he was taken over?' She sprang up. 'Come on!'

'Come on where?' That was Glitz.

'And, er, you're not really supposed to leave the room ...' put in Kade.

'We're going to talk to Triptolemos.'

'Why? Your theory is he doesn't remember what he did; he's not going to confess!' said Glitz.

'But we might be able to find out *something*.'

'All right,' said Kade reluctantly. 'We'll all go.'

'I'm not sure confronting him in here was the best move,' Glitz muttered to Mel as they entered the galley. 'I can count one ... two ... three ... oh, about 400 potential weapons.'

Mel was feeling equally wary. She'd been filled with the adrenalin of the investigation, but maybe it would have been sensible to invite Triptolemos to join them in a room with fewer blades, flames and blunt instruments.

'Melanie!' Triptolemos cried as he saw them. 'You are out of the rec room! That is good, very good. I have said to Livyia many times, "That Melanie, she could never hurt so much as a tiny, tiny fly. Do not keep her locked away! She, who made such a wonderful welcome meal for us all!"'

'Oh. Yes.' This was the opening Mel needed, but it was difficult. She gave an awkward cough. 'You know, Triptolemos, there was a point when I thought you weren't happy about me making the welcome meal, or being in the galley. You got this strange look on your face...'

The man held up a hand in front of him to hide his face from view. 'Oh, but I beg you do not mention that. I am ashamed – yes, so, so ashamed. It was the thought of a moment, and then it was gone – gone! Never to return.'

Mel swapped a confused look with Glitz. This wasn't what she'd expected at all.

He remembered that happening?

And... he really *had* been angry with her?

'You... were cross with me?' she said.

'And I am so ashamed!' he repeated. 'It is my galley, you see. My kitchen. I think always of it passing from the girl Charlie – the cook of Crew C – to me. Now I find she is dead, she cannot pass the kitchen to me, and suddenly there is in it an interloper – and I feel here –' he thumped his chest – 'a pain, and I wish you were not in my kitchen. I beg you to forgive me, for I know your actions were meant most kindly.'

'There's... there's nothing to forgive, Triptolemos,' said Mel. 'I was insensitive. I see that now. No –' as he was about to speak – 'please don't apologise again. I hadn't looked at it that way before, and I don't blame you at all for thinking like that.' She meant what she said. Her enthusiasm had carried her off, as it sometimes did. But his being genuinely upset with her didn't fit in with the picture they'd been painting. 'I'd just wondered... you don't have any blank spots in your memory? Say, times where you weren't sure how you got somewhere?'

'Ha ha!' boomed Triptolemos. 'You think I have been sampling too much of the gwampa juice? No no, I keep my mind clear as crystal always. A kitchen –' he said, waving a cleaver in the air and making them all take a step back – 'is a place most dangerous, and I wish there to be no accidents!'

'Do you think that was supposed to be a threat?' asked Mel, when she, Glitz and Kade were back in the rec room.

'No,' said Kade immediately. He seemed to have become part of their gang now. 'That was just Triptolemos.'

'So maybe my hypnotism theory *doesn't* work after all.'

'But it's the only thing that *does* make sense!' cried Kade. 'Our crew was created to work together in absolute harmony. We couldn't *kill* each other. We've never even had a disagreement!'

'Well, that is darn tootin' impossible,' said Glitz. 'You've had five years or more with these people and never a single disagreement? What if one of you wants to watch astro-ball on TV and the other –' he shot a look at Mel – 'wants to watch zero-gravity cats?'

'And you have had disagreements!' said Mel. 'Vizhan had a go at Nash about the chemicals. Frog got upset with Demarr for monopolising Nash! And ...' She trailed off.

'Looks like you've got three murder victims and one common factor there ...' pointed out Glitz.

Nash. But Mel really liked them!

'None of those disagreements would be motives for murder,' she protested.

Glitz looked uncomfortable. 'It can be the little things that niggle…'

'I suppose so. Like when a Navarino steps on your toe and you try to garotte him.'

Glitz threw his hands up in the air. 'Must you fling instances from my delinquent youth in my face, Melanie?'

'It was last July!'

'Delinquent middle age, then! The point is, such happenings are in the past.'

Mel sighed. 'And *these* deaths are entirely in the present.'

'Could Nash have done it, though?'

'Committed the crimes? They were already on the list of possibles for Vizhan's murder – if we're assuming now that Vizhan was the intended victim after all. For the second murder… well, remember what Bastelle said. He, Frog and Pearleye were in and out of the shuttle bay right up to the time Frog suited up, so one of them would have seen any incomers. Well, maybe they did. Maybe Nash went in when Frog was there. Frog wouldn't suspect anything – and obviously couldn't tell anyone afterwards. Then with Demarr – well, I'm afraid the whole scheme with the "paws" joke and being gassed has always been suspicious. Pretending to be a victim is a classic move. And there'd be no problem getting Demarr to go with them into the garden. Yes. It all works. I think it has to be Nash.'

Kade's face was a void, a place of hollowness. He'd been following their arguments, even offering help, but this was too much for him.

'I'm so sorry,' Mel said softly, but he didn't react. 'I know it's a shock …' she tried. Still nothing.

Glitz put his finger to his lips, and produced a key. He gestured to the door.

'Did you just pick the pocket of a devastated man?' hissed Mel.

Kade started sobbing. Then he slowly collapsed until he was leaning heavily on Mel.

'Um … struggling to breathe here!' she said.

A clearly irritated Glitz heaved Kade off her, and drew him to his feet. 'Come on, old son,' he said, gruffly. 'Let's get you some help.'

'Not Nash!' Mel cried.

'Do I have porridge for a brain? Of course not. I'll take him to the flight deck. And explain all of …' He clearly couldn't find words to encompass the situation. 'And explain.'

Mel didn't move after Glitz and Kade had gone. She was playing back every interaction with Nash she'd had – anything that might offer proof for what was just a hypothesis.

A hypothesis that fitted all the facts, true – but however compelling, it was worthless without evidence.

How long had she been sitting there when the sound of an opening door drew her from her brown study? She looked up, expecting to see Glitz returning.

But the person entering the room was Nash.

'Bastelle said you were all alone, so I thought I'd come and keep you company.'

Mel knew that couldn't be true. Even if Bastelle had said something along those lines – which seemed unlikely – Glitz would have made sure that she wasn't left vulnerable like this.

Nash locked the door behind them. 'Sorry,' they said. 'I think it's ridiculous, but it's the rules. I actually argued with Livyia about it. She told me she likes you and finds it hard to believe you've had any part in this – but her responsibility is to the sleepers.'

'I can understand that,' said Mel cautiously. Make them see you as a real person. Wasn't that the advice given to people in this sort of situation?

Nash was by the arcade machine. The arcade machine was by the door. She could bang on it and scream – but they wouldn't let her get that far. She subtly switched positions so the table was between her and Nash; if nothing else it might hold them off for a few moments if they attacked.

The worst thing was, Mel had liked Nash. Really liked them. She felt varying degrees of fondness towards the – still living – members of Crew D, with Caleb, Pearleye and Bastelle at the bottom end and Triptolemos, Kade, Livyia and Nash having real friend potential, under other circumstances. Admittedly, one of the things she'd liked most about Nash was that they clearly didn't believe she could have hurt anyone – not quite such a major factor if they were the murderer all along!

'Nash,' she said. 'I just wanted to thank you.'

'For what?'

'For showing me kindness, despite this suspicion hanging over us – despite you having lost your friends. It would probably have been easier for everyone to lock up the three of us and throw away the key. But I know *all my friends*, all the people I care about would be grateful to you too. Let me tell you about my friend, the Doctor, and all the things we did together …'

It was working! She could see it was working!

Nash was interested – was getting invested in her stories! Mel was becoming Scheherazade, telling tales to extend her life. And she had enough tales to keep them going well into old age! She'd had a copy of the *One Thousand and One Nights* at home; the picture of Scheherazade on the cover had looked rather like Vizhan.

Perhaps foolishly, she mentioned that.

'Who?' asked Nash.

Mel just stared for a moment. What did that mean? Was Nash blanking out the memories of their crimes somehow, or just playing with her?

'You know – Vizhan! Tall, dark, really pretty …'

'Are you thinking of the captain?' Nash asked. 'She's tall, dark and pretty, but her name's Livyia.'

'No, I'm not thinking of the captain.' This was bizarre. 'Vizhan was the ship's horticulturist.'

'You really are confused,' said Nash. 'Hope Kolahra is the ship's horticulturist.'

'Hope's only been on board a couple of days! She came with me and Glitz, we rescued her from – well, never mind about that, the point is that she hadn't even seen a carrot until two days ago. She's certainly not a horticulturist!'

Now it was Nash who was looking confused. 'That doesn't make sense,' they said.

Mel's mind was racing. She'd given up her theory about people on the *Kazemi* being controlled somehow, but maybe that had been right all along!

'What about the others?' she asked. 'Frog and Demarr? Do you remember them?'

Nash's face was veering towards anger now. 'I'm hardly likely to forget them, am I? They were like family!' Their tone hardened. 'I've been defending you, Mel. Pushing for everyone to treat you with kindness and understanding. I thought I was a good judge of people, and that you were a good person. And now you're playing some kind of ridiculous game. I don't even get why. Are you just trying to mess with me?'

'No! No, of course not! Please, Nash, could we try to talk about this? Because, I promise, I *am* a good person – or at least I try to be. I'm definitely not perfect! But there's something very odd going on on this ship, and maybe together we could work it out.'

But the anger wasn't going away. Nash was leaning against the arcade machine; Mel could see their fists were clenching.

She began to feel scared again.

Her eyes darted around for anything she could use to defend herself. But she didn't dare look away from Nash for long.

Mel knew she had to be ready to react. Nash wasn't very big or bulky, and Mel was fast, but speed wouldn't give her an edge in a small, locked room …

There was a sound at the door, and it opened. Bastelle came in.

The relief! Mel let out so much breath that she actually felt her body deflating.

'Oh, Bastelle,' she said as he shut the door behind him. 'You remember Vizhan, don't you?'

'Of course!' he said.

'Well, Nash says they don't remember her!'

He looked at Nash, who looked back at him. 'You don't remember her at all, TC?'

'No,' said Nash, shaking their head. 'I don't understand …'

Bastelle took their hand. 'I'll see what I can do about that,' he said.

And then his other hand went around Nash's throat, and he slammed their head down on the arcade cabinet.

Chapter Sixteen
Unforgettable

It was one of those moments where life changes. The world goes from before to after so quickly that it's impossible to isolate the tipping point in the middle. Mel felt afterwards that she should have prevented it, but even with her camera-like mind rewinding frame by frame, she could see no moment where that would have been possible.

Nash, lying on the floor.

Rewind.

Their head connecting with the cabinet.

Rewind.

Bastelle, pushing their head down.

Rewind.

Bastelle, reaching for their throat ...

Mel blinked, and she was back in the present, with Nash lying on the floor and Bastelle standing over them.

She screamed and ran for the door.

But Bastelle had locked it. Now he was on top of her, and Mel braced herself for the blow – but he just grabbed her by the arm and threw her away from him. While she lay dazed on the floor, he unlocked the door and fled through it. It slammed shut.

Why? Why had he done this? *Bastelle?* She'd never suspected him, not once. She wasn't sure she'd ever seen him so much as talk to Vizhan or Frog or Demarr; this was probably the first time she'd seen him talk to Nash!

Mel tried to pull herself up, but she was dizzy and disoriented. And there, at her feet, lay the body.

There wasn't much blood. But Nash's eyes were wide and staring. Accusing. Their face was in front of her wherever she looked, floating in her vision, looking so hurt: *You could have saved me, Mel. This is your fault, Mel. You should have worked it out sooner, Mel.*

Mel had seen death so often now. The sheer horror of that instant when a person, someone who'd been a baby, a little child, their mother's darling, someone who'd experienced their first kiss, their first love, who'd chosen their path in life, who'd experienced moment after moment of happiness, sadness, fun, laughter, envy, contentment, misery, anxiety, fulfilment – when that person became nothing. All those years, months, weeks, days, hours, brought to a sudden, irreversible end. Turned into a thing, that would never feel anything again, would never *be* again.

Mel was a happy person. Because she liked *being*. Even in the midst of horrors, she was filled with a love of existence.

What was it Glitz had said of her only the day before? *It's been less than twenty-four Earth-standard hours since she last offered to sacrifice her own life to save someone else, which is a thing she has done on many previous occasions.* That wasn't because she didn't want to go on living. It was because she loved life so much. She couldn't bear to see it taken away from anyone, and if she could stop that – even at the ultimate cost to herself – she would. She thought back to Captain Kolahra's log: *Not one of us could bear to feed our own bellies while a child hungers. One of the first things we did on arrival here was to switch off the ship's conscience machine in order to conserve power. But this is proof that no such machine was ever needed. There is no higher priority in anyone's mind than our children's futures.*

Yes, Captain Kolahra would have understood.

Even so, Mel never detached herself from the reality of death. The shock was pounding at her brain, inserting itself into every part of her. She knew she had to keep going, had to get after Bastelle. But she couldn't find a way of making that happen ...

The door was flung open, and Caleb and Pearleye stormed in. The sight of Nash's body brought them up short – but then they visibly collected themselves and stomped over to Mel. Caleb grabbed her left arm and Pearleye her right, his hand connecting just where Bastelle had grabbed her before. She yelped in pain. He only gripped her harder.

'I didn't do this!' Mel gasped. 'It was Bastelle, I saw him ...' Part of her was rolling its eyes, telling her that defending herself before anyone had even accused her made her look guilty, but she couldn't help it. She knew where this was going, had known even before she saw the expressions on Caleb and Pearleye's faces. Why else would Bastelle have left her alive?

They pulled her to her feet and took her to the flight deck. She wasn't sure if she walked or they dragged her, or if she stumbled along in a mixture of both. It all felt unreal.

Everyone was on the flight deck, Bastelle standing beside the captain.

'I'm sorry, Mel,' Livyia said. 'I've tried all the way through to give you the benefit of the doubt. But you must see that's no longer possible. Not with an eyewitness. I just want to understand why – why you want to endanger our mission.'

'Didn't – do it,' choked Mel. 'Not me – Bastelle.'

The captain's eyes hardened. 'I understand that earlier you accused Nash of perpetrating these crimes. And now you say it's Bastelle!'

So Glitz – or Kade – had told Livyia her suspicions. She looked around for them. There! Kade looked as though he was himself again. And Glitz would stick up for her. He knew she could never kill anyone – could never even *hurt* anyone!

But … the way Glitz just glanced at her. Like he didn't know her, like she was nothing. 'There's clearly no question that Mel killed Nash,' he said. 'But I believe she was genuinely convinced that Nash was responsible for the earlier murder, that of Demarr. Perhaps she felt, wrongly or rightly, that her own life was in danger.'

That was *Glitz* talking? No … How …?

'I will *never* believe that TC Nash killed anyone,' growled Pearleye.

'They didn't,' Mel tried again. 'It was Bastelle...'

'But Mel isn't part of the crew,' Glitz continued. 'She doesn't understand the absolute loyalty between crew-members – that there's never been so much as a cross word between any of us.'

Mel just gaped. Glitz wasn't part of the crew either! And he knew as well as anyone that what he'd just said wasn't true.

'But there *have* been cross words between members of the crew!' she cried. 'Don't you remember Vizhan getting angry with Nash about chemicals, or Frog being upset with Demarr at the welcome meal?'

'Who?' asked Livyia. 'I mean, Demarr I know, but—'

'Vizhan – your horticulturist. And Frog, your flight engineer!'

The captain sighed. 'I don't know what game you're playing, but our horticulturist is Hope Kolahra, and our flight engineer is Sabalom Glitz.'

'That's not right,' said Mel. She looked around – there was Kade; *he* remembered Vizhan, they'd talked about her... 'Kade! I know you're upset at what we thought we'd discovered, but you must tell the captain about Vizhan!'

He looked at her for a few seconds – then turned to the captain. 'Something's affecting her brain.'

'Come here,' said the captain. Nervously, Mel obeyed. Livyia tapped on the keyboard and brought up the ship's manifest.

Kazemi Crew D:
Captain: Livyia Terle.
Pilot: Rufus Kade.
First Officer: Heide Demarr (deceased).
Flight Engineer: Sabalom Glitz.
Systems Specialist: Rom Bastelle.
Life Systems: Caleb Havermine.
Cook: Triptolemos.
Medical Officer: TC Nash (deceased).
Horticulturist: Hope Kolahra.
Security: Suim Pearleye.

There were even headshots of Glitz and Hope – clearly taken recently, unlike the others, which showed the crewmembers as several years younger, but Mel suspected that no one would care if she tried to tell them that. If they didn't even remember the kerfuffle at the welcome meal …

There's never been so much as a cross word between any of us.

Every member of the crew is utterly trustworthy.

Our crew was created to work together in absolute harmony. We've never even had a disagreement!

And then an idea popped into Mel's head. She would have preferred if it had occurred to her when she'd had the time to think it through properly, but …

She'd come to the conclusion that Nash was the killer because they'd been the only linking factor in all the suspicious events.

Vizhan had shouted at Nash about chemicals.

Frog had been angry with Demarr for monopolising Nash.

Nash had been embarrassed by Demarr's 'inappropriate behaviour'.

Now, with Nash's innocence proved, she added another to the list: Nash had 'had words' with the captain about her treatment of Mel.

There'd been negativity towards Mel or Glitz or Hope – the incomers – but these were the only occasions Mel was aware of where a crewmember had been upset with another crewmember. And each person murdered had been *the source of* the negativity.

If you displayed anger towards another crewmember… you died.

Because there must be no cross words between crewmembers. They must work in absolute harmony.

It was essential for the mission to have a devoted crew.

A crew of *a minimum of eight people.*

'We can't add you to the system. It's crewmembers only.'

The only person who can add anyone to the system is Bastelle.

Bastelle is in charge of the system.

Or is the system in charge of Bastelle…?

Get rid of the angry crewmembers. But there has to be a minimum of eight people on the system.

Livyia, Kade, Demarr, Frog, Bastelle, Caleb, Triptolemos, Nash, Vizhan, Pearleye: Ten.

Livyia, Kade, Demarr, Frog, Bastelle, Caleb, Triptolemos, Nash, Pearleye: Nine.

Livyia, Kade, Demarr, Bastelle, Caleb, Triptolemos, Nash, Pearleye: Eight.

Livyia, Kade, Bastelle, Caleb, Triptolemos, Nash, Pearleye: Seven.

That wasn't enough. So at some point, the system had been overwritten. Maybe all at once, or person by person, Vizhan had been erased from the crew's minds and replaced with Hope.

So Livyia, Kade, Bastelle, Caleb, Triptolemos, Nash, Pearleye: Seven. But add Hope: Eight.

Livyia, Kade, Bastelle, Caleb, Triptolemos, Pearleye, Hope: Seven.

Not enough again. So add Glitz: Eight.

What if someone else dies?

Add Mel: Eight.

No. They weren't taking away her independence. They weren't taking away her individuality – her *memory*! She had to get out of here before another spat came along and Bastelle got homicidal again …

Even now, Bastelle was saying, 'Remember, Captain, you have the authority to order an execution.'

'No!' cried Mel. 'No, no!'

The witch hunt had started again. And even Glitz and Hope were joining in now. *Witch witch witch witch …*

Chapter Seventeen
Law & Order

'For the safety of the mission, Captain ...'

'She could be a danger to us, Captain ...'

'She could be a danger to the millions in the microstore, Captain ...'

'We can't risk it, Captain ...'

Mel tried to interject again and again, but it was as though she wasn't there.

She needed a friend.

She needed Glitz – or Hope.

She needed Nash, who'd fought for her.

The only friend she could think of now was ...

Barry Day!

But if Bastelle was behind everything, he could have hidden that tiny yellow cube anywhere on the ship.

'You're all correct,' said the captain. 'I cannot endanger our mission any further. But I do believe there is at least a possibility that Mel may have killed in what she thought was self-defence. Therefore, I will not approve an execution.'

Mel started shaking with relief.

'Instead, Mel is to be put in suspended animation, until the end of the journey.'

'No!' Mel gasped. 'You can't do that! Please, if you'd just listen to me …'

But they still weren't listening. They weren't even acknowledging her.

She had to get away. *Barry!* Where could that cube be? No one could access the airlock without other people knowing – the captain had put measures in place after Frog's death to ensure that – so it must still be on the ship. But there were a million places it could be. Barry himself had found potential secret hiding places all over the ship! And even without those, it would be close to impossible to track it down. The garden alone would take days to search thoroughly, and as for the engineering section …

To say it was like looking for a needle in a haystack was something of an understatement.

But there was a difference between Barry Day and a needle.

You couldn't wake up a needle!

Mel let herself go limp. Utterly despondent. The picture of hopelessness, a woman who was completely defeated.

So that no one was expecting it when she ran, off from a standing start faster than Colin Jackson. And she didn't aim for the door, as they might have expected.

She hit the captain's intercom button so her voice would be relayed all over the ship. 'Barry! Wake up! *Wake up!*'

She held her breath. Barry would save her. Barry would save her!

Nothing.

'Let's get this over with,' said Livyia, not unkindly. 'Caleb, Pearleye...'

The two men took her arms again, and she was too defeated to even think of resisting. Suspended animation – well, it wasn't that bad. She was so far from her own time and place that a few hundred years here or there wouldn't make a lot of difference. At least she'd still be Melanie Bush when she woke up, unlike poor Glitz and Hope, who'd been robbed of half their identities.

She wouldn't see either of them again, of course. The crew knew they would die of old age if nothing else before the ship's journey was complete. If there were no more murders, Hope might actually have a good life. The crew thought of themselves as a family, and a family was what she needed. Glitz, though...

Oh, she would miss Glitz.

Caleb and Pearleye led her off the flight deck, the rest of the crew following behind. They were heading for the hydroponic garden, presumably for the awakening chamber or even the microstore beyond it.

They stepped into the garden...

'You're mistreating Mel! Squixy's gonna go...'

Mel looked up with delight. '*Nuts!*'

221

The Squirrel Shuttle hurtled overhead, roaring loudly. Acorn bombs rained down all around – and exploded!

Boom boom boom!

Caleb and Pearleye let go of Mel's arms. There were flashes and bangs and clouds of purple smoke – the rest of the crew were calling out, angry and confused, as Mel took to her heels.

There was so much noise, so much confusion. But Barry led her on a safe path through the plants.

'In here!' he said.

There was nothing there. Was the escape over already?

'Come on, lass – it's one of the service hatches I found!' And he showed her exactly where it was, and how to get in, and suddenly she was … safe.

Safe!

For now, at least.

'Squixy'll hold 'em off,' Barry told her, and she could hear the continuing explosions of acorn bombs, muffled now. 'She won't hurt anyone – but they're not to know that.'

'Thank you,' said Mel, as she regained her breath. She frowned, looking closer at Barry in the dim light. 'Have you dyed your hair?'

'No! But someone stuck my cube in a jar of potassium permanganate in the medic's room. Now everything I touch turns purple.'

Mel almost giggled, but the situation was too serious. 'This service duct,' she said. 'Does anyone else know that it's here?'

'Maybe,' said Barry. 'I found it on the system, so ...'

'So anyone else connected to the system can find it too. Which I imagine is everyone now.' Mel sighed. And then she realised something. 'When we wanted to access the shuttles, you told us that people had to be manually added to the system.'

'That's right, lass.'

'So Bastelle must have added Glitz and Hope to the system.'

'Sounds right to me.'

'Can you remove them from the system?'

'Me? No. They have to be—'

'Manually removed? I thought as much. So ... let's go and manually remove them.'

'You mean ...?'

'You and me, Barry. We're going to smash the system!'

Mel would have given a sizeable fortune for a pair of knee pads. She and Barry had been crawling through the service tunnels for ages. She was tired, cramped and thirsty, and was beginning to think that a century or so in suspended animation would at least offer a nice rest. They had to go slowly in order to be quiet, and anything but the occasional whisper was too risky. Mel's main fear was that Bastelle would anticipate her course of action and be waiting for her – but luckily they had a puppet squirrel to scout ahead. After her acorn-bombing was done, Squixy had joined them in the tunnels, and was proving invaluable.

'Squeak squeak!'

'All clear,' translated Barry. 'Come on, lass!'

Mel quietly removed an access panel and slid into a bay. Her legs had forgotten how to stay straight and keep her upright, and she had to spend a couple of minutes bent over until they remembered. 'This is it, then, is it?' she said. The system was the size of two or three wardrobes and looked as solid and secure as a bank vault. 'How do I get into this?'

'I'll get you the codes,' said Barry, and his eyes rolled back into his head as his AI brain sent out feelers to grab that knowledge.

What was inside the vault was much more complex than Mel had anticipated, and she had no idea how to get started. 'What would happen if I just started smashing it up?' she asked. 'What if I pulled out a load of wires?'

'What d'you think, viewers?' asked Barry. 'Will Mel turn off the oxygen supply – or the artificial gravity? Vote now!'

'I'm taking that to mean it's not a great idea,' said Mel.

With Barry's help, she started to explore the system in detail. She needed to work out how to remove Glitz and Hope from it – without simultaneously killing them in some unfortunate way. 'What's this?' she asked.

She'd found a rectangular box deep inside the circuitry which didn't look like it belonged there. There was a symbol on the side: a straight horizontal line topped with another horizontal line with a hump in the middle. It looked familiar, but before she could locate it in her memory, Barry said, 'That's the astronomical symbol for the constellation Libra.'

'How odd,' said Mel. 'What do you know about Libra?'

Barry began to rattle off the names of stars and planets in the constellation, and their properties. None of it seemed relevant at all, and Mel started to tune it out, thinking through what *she* knew about the star sign.

And then, everything clicked into place.

'Libra,' she said. 'Symbolised by the scales of justice. As held by the Greek goddess Themis, the personification of moral order – the civilised behaviour required by the gods. There's a reason that negativity isn't allowed on this ship.'

'What's that?' asked Barry.

'The *Kazemi* has a conscience machine. Just like the *Seraphine*.'

Conscience machines were rare, but not so rare that finding them on two unrelated ships was wildly improbable. They were used to keep emotions balanced, flattening out extremes of both negativity and positivity and creating harmony. Both the *Seraphine* and the *Kazemi* were on long voyages, exactly the conditions where interpersonal issues, if they occurred, might be catastrophic. It was frowned upon for a machine to be used without the knowledge of those governed by it, but it certainly wasn't unknown.

Barry was frowning. 'I don't get it.'

'A conscience machine controls people's emotions. It can control people's minds!'

'Yeah, I get *that*, lass. It's just … you're saying negativity isn't allowed on this ship.'

'That's right.'

DOCTOR WHO

'But isn't murder ... kind of negative?'

Mel sighed. 'Yes, Barry. Yes, it is. I think something's gone very wrong with this particular conscience machine. Maybe that's what happens when one's left unmaintained for years and years.'

'So what are we gonna do about it?'

'We're going to switch it off!'

Mel's feisty declaration had filled her with a level of positivity that soon faded when she was met with the practicalities of the situation.

Of course, the box had nothing so straightforward as an actual on/off switch. She tried to work out a way to detach it from the surrounding circuitry, but it was enmeshed too deeply.

'Can I just destroy it?' she asked Barry. 'You know ... grab something and bash it into bits!'

Barry shrugged despondently. 'Sorry, lass. That'd take out half the system with it, and probably you too.'

'But there has to be a way! Captain Kolahra turned off the *Seraphine*'s conscience machine without blowing up himself or his ship!'

'Well, he was probably connected to it, lass. An authorised user, a sys-op!'

'Oh.' Mel thought about that for a moment. 'So if I want to switch it off – I have to join it? Become part of it?'

'Squeak!' Squixy snuggled up to Mel and shook her furry head fiercely.

226

'I know, Squixy, it doesn't seem like a good idea. If I join it, it might be able to control me. But I've got to give it a go.'

'*Squeak!*' The squirrel hopped up and down, waving her paws at Barry.

'Aye. I agree, Squixy.' Barry smiled his wonderful smile, and held out a hand to Mel. 'You're not going in alone, lass. We've got you.'

Mel smiled back. And took his hand.

Mel blinked, and she was elsewhere.

She was in what appeared to be a wireframe model of the *Kazemi*, a 3D representation created from lines of green drawn on solid black. Floating through it, she managed to identify shapes corresponding to all those she'd left behind: Glitz and Hope, Livyia, Caleb, Pearleye, Kade, Triptolemos. They moved around the net of the ship, presumably following the actions of the humans they represented.

Mel looked for Bastelle.

There he was, his line-sculpted avatar standing alone in the engine room – and suddenly there he was again, in full colour, floating in front of her. The Libra symbol swam over his head, like a stylised bicorne hat.

'Bastelle,' she said.

'No,' replied the figure, and she realised that the system had merely borrowed Bastelle's form to represent itself.

She said that, and added: 'But you've taken him over in real life, too, haven't you? You're controlling him. He's been murdering people because of you.'

227

'Harmony is essential.'

'No, harmony is desirable. Free will is essential … Yes, harmony is essential.'

Suddenly Barry's hand was on her shoulder, shaking her, and Mel realised that her opinion had changed even while she'd been talking.

No, it had *been changed* for her.

'Don't do that,' Mel told the system.

'The mission is more important than free will. I have 75 million lives to protect.'

'And how many of those would you rub out if they expressed an extreme emotion?'

Bastelle's face fizzed and distorted, one eye winking.

Mel felt a rush of sympathy. 'Oh, please listen to me,' she said. 'This isn't about right or wrong. It's about you *going* wrong. Something's happened to you.'

The face glitched again.

And then, the next moment, Mel was in another scene, another wireframe.

She couldn't instantly identify the shapes surrounding her, but finally realised that this was the supply station. One after another, ten 3D representations were dispatched into the rendered form of the *Seraphine*'s fuel tank.

But the screams that accompanied their demises weren't computer-generated.

They were as human as could be imagined.

After the tenth person had fallen to their death, the sequence started again.

'I'm so sorry,' whispered Mel. 'You were connected to all of them, weren't you?' That would be enough to drive anyone mad. Any*thing* mad.

'That's not the only problem,' said Barry. 'Oof! We've got a bit of corrosion in here! That's what fifteen years without maintenance can do to a circuit. Explains all the glitching.'

Fizz. Wink. Distort.

'And every time the conscience machine glitches, it lets a genuine human emotion get through!' It was all making sense to Mel now. 'Like Demarr falling for Nash, or Frog's jealousy – or Triptolemos resenting me being in his kitchen! I suppose it wasn't so much of a problem if it was aimed at someone outside the system like me – but you couldn't let there be negativity between your subjects. So you weeded out what you thought were the causes, the instigators of negativity. You killed them – using the poor man whose brain was plugged into you. Which was completely the right thing to do — *ouch!*'

Squixy's sharp rodent teeth had nipped her arm, and Mel realised how much danger she was in. She'd willingly walked into the lion's den.

This had to end, now.

'I'm shutting you down,' she told the machine. 'Barry? Take me in.'

The rock star held out a hand and, as Mel took it, numbers and letters began to appear in the air: a universe of code scrolling all around her.

Oh yes. She was on home territory now.

Mel dived into the flashing figures, rewriting them in her head and seeing them transform before her, creating a path that led her deeper and deeper into the machine's programming. The system tried to change them back and block her way, but Mel had Barry and Squixy and righteousness on her side.

And there it was. What she'd hoped to find.

The kill switch.

She reached out through the code …

… and the letters and numbers twisted into a rope, encircled her wrists, her ankles, her neck …

Mel tried to rewrite the code, but every push of her brain made the bonds tighten. And she was changing! The figures were transforming her, spreading through her like a virus. Her wrists were made of code, now her hands, now her arms … and then little chains of figures began to worm out of her, connecting her to the wireframes of the crew, to Glitz, to Hope, to Livyia …

'You can't shut me down,' said the system through Bastelle's mouth. 'You're part of me.'

'I'm so sorry, lass,' came Barry's voice. 'I thought I could keep you safe. But you're too entwined. If you operate the kill switch – you die too.'

Squixy was tugging at what had been Mel's hand, squeaking urgently.

'Squixy can show you the way out,' said Barry. 'Come back to us, Mel.'

'But the machine will just keep killing people!'

230

'I know. But at least you'll still be alive.'

'At what cost?' Mel drew in a deep breath, pulling hundreds of tiny green numbers into her proxy mouth and nose then exhaling them. With all her strength, she reached out for the kill switch.

A tiny thread of figures whipped around her waist, tugging her back. Then another, and another.

Not from Bastelle, not even from the code itself. Like a half-finished embroidery of many colours, each thread could be traced to a different origin. The golden silk that was Livyia, the red that came from Kade, the chestnut brown of Caleb. Pearleye was grey and Triptolemos was purple. Even Bastelle was part of it, his black code filaments barely showing against the black background. Hope reached out in cherry-blossom pink, and then there was Glitz, the dull copper of an old penny – or a grotzit. And voices snaked up every thread: *No. Let me.*

She tried again to move forward. 'They're not gonna let you, Mel,' said Barry. 'The system's in all of them, and you're in the system now. That means everyone's got a bit of Melanie Bush inside them. And you know what Melanie Bush would do in this situation. She'd sacrifice herself to save them all …'

'Well, I've had more than twenty years of being me,' said Mel. 'If I have to fight myself, I know who's going to win.'

And with the power of a woman who did at least an hour of aerobics every day, she pulled away and pressed the switch.

Chapter Eighteen
The Closer

For Mel, waking up in the small bunk room adjoining the medical centre was something of an anti-climax.

'She's awake!' yelled someone – Caleb, maybe, or Pearleye? – and a few moments later a sleepy Glitz stumbled in.

'We'd only just convinced him to get some sleep,' confided Kade, following him into the room. 'Would barely let you out of his sight the last couple of days.'

Mel laughed. 'What, Glitz?'

'Ignore this know-nothing dink,' mumbled that gentleman. 'Anyway, I needed to keep an orb on you. If you hadn't made it, I was planning to sue the makers of that conscience machine for a grotzit or two ...'

Kade rolled his eyes and twisted his face into a strange expression that Mel thought was trying to convey that she shouldn't believe a word of it. She laughed again. 'Sorry for preventing your payday, Glitz.'

He *hmph*ed.

'But – can you tell me what happened to me? Do you know? I … hit the kill switch …'

'Not quite.' The voice came from the doorway – Livyia. 'While you were taking on that machine, we were all given a little taste of what it's like to be Melanie Bush, and our first impulse was to sacrifice ourselves instead of you.' She took a chair by Mel's bedside. 'I hope you'll forgive me, Mel. I should have been able to see how honest you are. How good you are.'

Mel couldn't begin to respond to that. She knew she was blushing ferociously – and red cheeks did *not* go well with red hair.

'Good? Tell me about it!' muttered Glitz. 'Imagine living with all that altruism.'

'You didn't enjoy being me, then, Glitz?' Mel said with a cheeky grin.

'How *you've* stuck being you for twenty-odd years I'll never know,' he replied.

'But that was the key to the machine's destruction.' Livyia was speaking again. 'It was the last thing you said – that you'd been you for more than twenty years. Well, that's when he realised – we all felt it.'

'Er, who? And felt what?'

'That you had more experience of being Mel. Bastelle had more experience of being the system. He knew the way in, and he was the one who threw you out at the moment he hit the kill switch.'

'Oh.' Mel didn't ask if he'd survived. Their faces already told her the answer.

Livyia nodded. 'As I understand from Barry' – Barry grinned and waved – 'Bastelle used considerable psychic force to knock you away from the switch, and right out of the system itself. We don't have much experience of such matters, but it might take you some time to recover from that. I'm sorry … and I realise it will be hard for you to think kindly of him. You saw him kill Nash in front of your eyes. But I'd like you to know that I am certain Bastelle's sacrifice wasn't only down to your influence. He gave his life because without the connection to the damaged conscience machine, he was a good man. It was the real Bastelle who chose to save us all.'

Mel nodded. She wished she'd had the chance to meet that Bastelle. But at least now she could think of him without dwelling on the horror of what he'd done.

Mel hardly went five minutes without a visitor during the time she spent recuperating.

She was quite desperate to get out of bed, but Pearleye – now acting medical officer – insisted she rest. Triptolemos provided far too many 'oh-so-tempting' little meals, including, as a special treat, her 'favourite' fruit salad – recipe provided by Hope.

Rather like a small boy smuggling titbits to a dog underneath the dinner table, Mel sneaked the raw chilis out of her bowl and passed them to Squixy. Unfortunately, her subterfuge was discovered when Squixy turned fire-engine red and steam blew out of her ears.

The squirrel spent a lot of time cuddled up on Mel's pillow. Sometimes Mel wished it was Barry or even Kade there instead – but most of the time she was relieved that it was only a no-complications AI rodent. It was Squixy to whom Mel confided a great secret. She couldn't tell anyone, but a puppet squirrel – an unreal puppet squirrel at that – surely didn't count.

When Mel had been inside the code, the connections with the crew had gone both ways. She'd had a fleeting touch of everyone's minds. She hadn't remembered it at first; it was only when she saw someone that she'd suddenly get a flash of what she'd felt from them.

Without the conscience machine damping down their emotions, she'd understood that the steady Pearleye and the flamboyant, temperamental Triptolemos yearned for more of an attachment than regulations allowed. Kade, while happy and carefree, wished he'd been assigned to Crew M, where a sweet girl called Ada served as First Officer. Like a wartime lad lying about his age to join the army, Caleb had claimed to have no 'encumbrances', but Mel now knew his parents and younger brother and sister were among the sleepers in the microstore, and he wished he could see them again. Livyia was steadfast in her role as captain, but would have loved to help build the new society that awaited at the end of the journey.

She also knew that Hope wanted a home. And that Glitz ...

No. Glitz's thread had been far too tangled for her to read anything at all.

Mel's recuperation continued. Hope had been learning how to tend the plants in the hydroponic garden and seeing how much joy that brought her made Mel heal twice as fast (or so she insisted). Caleb and Pearleye told her a lot about their lives back on Earth and their hopes for its people's future, and Mel became fonder of them both by the day.

The crew avoided talking about the murders as much as possible, and it was days before Mel and Glitz were finally alone and could really discuss what had happened.

'Bastelle was in the medical centre with Hope when Vizhan argued with Nash,' said Mel. 'He must have taken the poison when everyone was distracted.'

'And the poison was in her goblet at the welcome meal?'

'Yes.' She nodded. 'Bastelle put the poison in Vizhan's goblet – they weren't glass so it didn't show. And everybody had taken a drink before Barry appeared, so it was her own goblet she drank out of, not mine.'

'You'd already got him on the list of people who could have killed Frog.'

'He was in and out of the shuttle bay all the time. And of course he was the person on watch outside the men's bunk room when Nash and I were knocked out. I said Nash was the obvious suspect, that they must have lured Demarr into the garden and killed her, then pretended to be unconscious – well, that worked just as well for Bastelle. And if he overheard Nash and me talking about fingerprints, framing you and me was child's play.'

'Talking of play…' Glitz got a pack of cards out of his pocket.

'Glitz, if you keep on with that, I'm going to move to Xuxion.'

'Xuxion? Why?'

'Because it's over eight light years from the nearest star casino, you said. And I am *not* going to be your stooge! Oh no.'

'What?'

'I saw that! You've just had an idea, haven't you? It's written all over your face!'

'Rubbish, Melanie,' Glitz insisted. Then a few seconds later, he casually announced, 'I might head off for a while. Let you rest.'

'I don't need rest and you've only just got here! Glitz, what are you up to?'

But of course, he didn't answer.

Finally came the grand day when Pearleye declared Mel could get up. Hope kept running in and out of the room while Mel was getting dressed. 'Are you ready yet?' she said every time. 'Are you ready yet? I'm supposed to take you to the flight deck.'

'Nearly there,' Mel assured her each time. She was dragging it out a bit. Hope's insistence made her wary that something awful awaited her, like a surprise party.

Unfortunately, her fears were confirmed. And it was even worse than she'd imagined.

There were cheers as she arrived and streamers were thrown, catching in her hair. Triptolemos had made a cake. 'A carrot cake, of course,' Glitz pointed out.

All that was embarrassing, but bearable. But then came the thing she hadn't been expecting. In front of everyone, Livyia came up to her.

'You've done so much for us already, Mel,' said the captain. 'But we all hope you will consider doing more. We would like you to stay. You and Glitz and Hope. Not just to replace the crewmembers we've lost, but to become part of our family.'

Mel gaped at her, then turned to Glitz and Hope – had they had any idea this was coming? Hope looked excited, Glitz looked – resigned? Was that it? She couldn't quite read his expression.

'If you want to leave, we'll understand, and let you have the shuttle, of course. But we hope you'll stay. After all, you're from Earth too. You have a stake in our mission. Please help to safeguard the future of our people – *your* people.'

The future of her people…

She should say yes. Livyia, Pearleye, Caleb, Triptolemos and Kade, and – yes, and Vizhan, Frog, Demarr and Nash too, to say nothing of Bastelle – they'd given up their personal desires for the good of everyone. What was in her future? Organising the *Tu-Two*, making deals and maybe, just maybe, making a difference…

What did any of that matter alongside this opportunity to *definitely* make a difference – for an entire civilisation!

'Please, Mel!' begged Hope.

But that moment when the *Nosferatu II* had arrived at the supply station, that moment when she and Glitz were about to christen Project *Tu-Two* – Mel had felt so excited.

She didn't feel excited now. *This* project lit no spark inside her.

Glitz cleared his throat. 'If it helps make up your mind,' he said, 'that shuttle's got my name on it. This isn't the place for me. Where's the profit to be found if you're stuck with the same people every single day till you die? Mind you,' he continued, 'at least that's better than surviving the journey and ending up on that hellhole Ravolox again.'

'Oh, it can't be as bad as you paint it,' said Caleb. 'It's our planet, it's where our people belong.'

A grin spread across Glitz's face. 'I thought someone might say that. So with the help of my artificially intelligent friend Mr Barry Day, I've arranged another little welcome-back surprise for Mel.' He adopted a showman's tone. 'If you'll all take your seats! OAPs and under-fives half-price, and why not treat yourself to a bag of nuts for the interval from our lovely usherette Miss Squixy Squirrel?'

Bewildered, the crew allowed themselves to be ushered to chairs.

'Lights please!' called Glitz.

The flight deck lights dimmed, and the largest computer screen blinked on, showing a wooded area.

A young man, bearded, wearing a silver jerkin, said, 'Well, they're not from around here, Mr Glitz.'

'*I know that, Dibber,*' came a voice they all recognised.

'Glitz, what is this?' Mel asked. And then someone else appeared on the screen. A tall man with fair curls and the most ridiculously colourful clothes ever assembled. 'That's the Doctor!' she cried in absolute delight.

'It is indeed the momentous first meeting between your Gallifreyan gentleman friend and myself,' Glitz agreed.

'Oh! So if this is when you first met ... It must be ...'

'Ravolox!' Glitz completed her sentence.

'It doesn't look *that* awful,' said Mel. 'But how are we seeing this? Oh.' She put her hands on her hips and tutted. 'This is part of the evidence from the Doctor's trial, isn't it?'

'It is.'

'Glitz – did you illegally download this from the Matrix?'

'Well,' he said, with a careless wave of his hand. 'Not as such, no. It had already been downloaded by another person involved in that legal caper. I merely copied it across onto a device of my own.'

'Oh Glitz!' She thought she knew who Glitz might have copied the file from, a certain person known as the Valeyard. Luckily, he was now history. And while being a witness at the Doctor's trial for his life hadn't been much fun, it was there that she first met Glitz, and the seeds of her current life were sown. For good or ill ...

She turned her attention back to the screen, not wanting to miss a second of the Doctor. How funny to think that she'd worried about the AI taking on his persona, because she thought it might dilute her own. She knew now that her fears were unfounded. She was Melanie Bush, and she would remain 100 per cent Melanie Bush. Oh, the Doctor had such a huge personality that it overshadowed those around him. She knew that. She wasn't planning to compete with him, or anyone else. She was just going to shine her own little light, so she could always be seen, even if other people were casting huge shadows.

This is what she'd really needed. To see the Doctor again – so she could see herself clearly too. What a wonderful gift from Glitz.

She realised something else, as the film came to an end and the flight deck lights were switched back on. The Doctor merrily went through life pointing other people in the right direction. Mel had always wondered how he found the confidence to do so. The confidence to interfere. The confidence that it *was* the right direction.

Watching him now, she realised that maybe he'd just learned to trust his instincts.

Well, she had instincts too.

And maybe her guess was as good as anyone's.

'You shouldn't go to Ravolox,' she said – so confidently, so forcefully, that everyone in the room turned to her.

'We don't deviate from the course,' said the entire crew in harmony – and then looked at each other, confused.

'Just hear me out,' said Mel. 'It's not because Ravolox couldn't be a great place. I know you'd sort it out – well, those of you who get there would. And that's the thing. There might only be eighty-five people left in the crews, compared with 75 million others. But I think the eighty-five should have a chance of a new life too. To be with each other. To be with your families. To make *new* families.'

'Mel, we've already explained, we're willing—'

'I know you're willing! That makes it worse! You're the sort of principled, upright people that a new colony really needs. And it should be a new colony, not just Earth Mark Two. Or rather, Earth Mark One, that's just in a different place.'

'But that is our destination!' exploded Triptolemos. 'That is where we are supposed to go – that is the only place we *can* go to, the only place that can support us!'

'It's not, you know,' said Glitz. 'I've been having a bit of a think about that. I reckon that when the Earth was dragged through the universe, it elbowed out everything that was already there, creating huge swathes of uninhabited space, and nothing good enough for you this side of Ravolox. But as the years went on, it all drifted back into place. Trouble is, it seems one of the little tricks of your conscience machine was not letting anyone even consider deviating from the mission. Now it's kaput, your options have just opened up! Mel, got that galactic gazetteer on you?'

'Of course I haven't,' she said. 'Don't you know everything that's happened to me since I left the *Tu-Two*?'

'Well, never mind,' said Glitz. 'This would not be the first planet I've sold sight unseen. We're talking no previous owners, we're talking breathable atmosphere, we're talking fertile soil, we're talking already approved for colonisation …'

Mel laughed. She knew now the thought that had come into Glitz's mind the other day when they'd been talking about Xuxion. 'And as an added bonus,' she said, 'we're talking eight light years from the nearest star casino.'

Chapter Nineteen

Life

'You don't have to,' said Mel. 'Livyia said she'd do the talking. Or I will, if you'd prefer – not they're likely to listen to me.'

Hope was visibly shivering. 'It has to be me,' she said. 'It's my …'

'Don't say "destiny"!' begged Mel.

'No,' said Hope. 'It's my … responsibility. I'm the baby of the beacon, after all. I'm supposed to show the way.'

'That sounds exactly like something Captain Kolahra's daughter would say,' said Mel.

Hope stopped shivering, and pulled herself to her full height. 'Yes,' she said. 'And I'm going to finish what my father started. I'm going to get everyone safely to Xuxion.'

She opened the door, and stepped onto the trading floor of the supply station.

* * *

The children of the *Seraphine* had lost their zealousness and fire.

To Mel's great relief, they hadn't starved without a working vending machine, but the provisions they'd harvested from some abandoned spacecraft were running low. Hope's offering of fruit and vegetables from the *Kazemi*'s hydroponic garden had been greeted initially with suspicion, but hunger overcame their distrust and they were soon begging for more.

'There's a way to get as much of it as you like,' Hope told them. 'All you have to do is come to Xuxion – as you've always wanted – and help grow it.'

'We're not going to Xuxion without Finrae!' shouted a young woman Mel recognised as one of Finrae's acolytes – June Terrij, according to Hope. 'What have you done with him?'

Mel turned to Glitz. 'Finrae's not here!' she whispered. 'The teleport bangle didn't bring him back!'

Glitz looked rather shifty. 'I, er… think it did,' he said. 'No!' he added, raising a hand to stop Mel commenting. 'None of my doing, honest, guv. Trouble is, pressing that button just gave him a return ticket to where we'd come from. It would've pulled him right back to the focus – your headset.'

'My headset?' Mel thought for a moment, and then saw it clearly in her memory: the headset tumbling off her head into the hell that was the *Seraphine*'s fuel tank.

'Oh,' she said. 'I don't think we'd better tell them that …'

The crowd was getting restless, and Mel could see that Hope was beginning to lose her nerve. There was a rumbling undercurrent of speech and one word kept cropping up: Finrae. *Finrae, Finrae, Finrae …*

Mel stepped forward. 'Finrae isn't coming back!' she announced. 'But he has been preparing you for this moment for years! You just didn't quite understand. Listen.' And she began to recite the words Finrae had said before each sacrifice:

'You become stardust
and fuel our ship with your sacrifice,
so it does not hunger
and does not hurt.
When the ship is full
and hope is with you at last,
we will all meet at journey's end.'

Mel called for Barry to join her. 'Barry, could you explain to these people what stardust is?'

'Of course, lass. David Bowie's "Starman" alter ego was—'

'Not *Ziggy* Stardust. *Actual* stardust.'

'Got you, lass! Stardust is tiny cosmic particles.'

'Which could form, or be formed by, a meteor storm?'

'That sort of thing, aye.'

'So those meteors *sacrificed* themselves to crash the *Seraphine* and, er –' she was making this up as she went along and her reasoning wouldn't stand up to any scrutiny, but if she spoke confidently enough it might just work – 'that all ultimately led to the arrival of the *Kazemi*, a ship that has food and medical supplies so you won't hunger or hurt. And the *Kazemi* is very full – it has over 75 million people on board! Now Hope has returned to you, at last, and all those 75 million people will awaken to meet you at journey's end – Xuxion.'

Were they buying it? She wasn't sure.

Then Hope spoke again. 'Thank you, Mel. Thank you for trying to help us. But we don't have to justify Finrae's words. We have to accept that they were wrong. That everything we've done and believed has been wrong, for years. Please, all of you – put the past beside you, and join me on the *Kazemi* – and on Xuxion.'

It was the Watcher of the Arrow who first came to stand by Hope.

Then another of the cultists, and another.

Those who'd been Finrae's acolytes held back at first, but whether from conviction or hunger or fear of being left alone, they joined the party in the end.

'We're all going to Xuxion!' Hope cried, and they joined in the cheer.

'We're all going to Xuxion!'

Hope went back to her cabin on the *Seraphine*, accompanied by Mel. Livyia had asked for all of Hope's embroideries. With those, and the IDs of the spaceships in the ship's graveyard around the beacon, she planned to reach out and give closure to anyone who might still be waiting for a ship to come home.

'I don't think I'm going to stitch any more pictures,' Hope told Mel, as she picked up the tin of silks that had once been her mother's. 'Or not yet, anyway. But I did make just one more embroidery.'

The girl took something out of her pocket. She seemed nervous – so nervous that she couldn't even make eye contact.

'Pearleye found me the silks,' she said. 'Well, they weren't proper silks, they're called "sutures"; we got them from the medical bay and we coloured them with berry juice and things from the garden.'

She held it out.

It was a square of material, not much bigger than the one that said HOPE, which they'd put up on the wall above the berth that had been Vizhan's and would be Hope's until they arrived on Xuxion. This one also said HOPE – but added some other words too.

'"Never lose Hope",' Mel read. 'That's lovely.'

'And that's me,' said the girl, pointing to an embroidered figure with long plaited hair. 'And the green is the garden I'm going to make on Xuxion. Oh, and those are the carrots I'm going to grow too. To remember you by.'

'As long as you don't put them in a fruit salad,' Mel decided *not* to say. What she did say was, 'Thank you, Hope. I'll treasure it.'

Hope's embroidery wasn't the only souvenir of the adventure that Mel would treasure. The last person she said goodbye to, before the *Kazemi* left and she and Glitz set off up the relocated chute to the *Nosferatu II*, was Barry Day. Or, if you counted Squixy, who was sitting on his shoulder, the last *two* people.

Barry had taken on the role of Systems Specialist for the final part of the *Kazemi*'s journey. They'd transferred ownership of the interface to Hope. As Glitz had warned Mel in the first place, the AI couldn't take on a new persona, but everyone seemed perfectly happy to accept a rock-star TV presenter from 1980 as a member of their new colony.

'Got something for you, lass.'

Mel was half expecting to be presented with a Pretenders LP – or maybe, just maybe, a kiss. But it was better than either of those things. A 'Squixy's Space Squad' badge was one thing, but the 'Squixy's SUPER SPECIAL Space Squad' *medal* that the squirrel placed around Mel's neck was something else.

'It's the only one that's ever been awarded,' Barry told her.

'I'm going to miss you, Barry,' said Mel.

'Squeak!'

'And you too, of course, Squixy.'

Barry gave her that heart-melting lopsided smile. 'Could I just ask you one thing before we say goodbye, lass?'

She couldn't look away from his brilliant blue eyes. 'Yes, Barry. Of course. Anything.'

He reached out a hand and lightly touched her hair. 'Mel …'

'Yes, Barry?'

'What shampoo do you use? The onboard atmosphere's really drying out me hair and I've started getting split ends.'

And then, finally, they were back on the *Nosferatu II*.

'Oh, you wonderful, darling ship,' crooned Glitz. 'I'll never leave you again.'

'I think you might have to,' said Mel, although she was going through similar emotions. 'That wasn't a particularly profitable beginning for Operation *Tu-Two*.'

'Really?' said Glitz. '*You* might not have achieved much in the finance department, but I'm ahead by several thousand grotzits.

Mel gaped. 'How?'

'Remember I explained to you how potential buyers at the supply station had to lodge their funds before trading to dodge the dirty rotten scoundrels who might have half-inched their goods and chattels?'

'Yes,' said Mel, who thought she knew where this was going.

'Well, since no trade happened for obvious, engine-feeding reasons, and since the prospective tradespeople were too dead to embark on the refund process ... Out of the goodness of my heart, I decided to straighten out their accounts for them. Your friend Barry Day kindly accessed the computer system and facilitated my magnanimous gesture.'

'Exactly how magnanimous?' Mel asked.

'Oh, about 48,219 grotzits worth of magnanimity.'

'That's wonderful!' said Mel. 'I never dreamed we'd get anywhere near our first target of 50,000 grotzits this quickly!'

'Our … first target?'

'For our first project! Oh Glitz, I've shown you all the paperwork, all my plans …'

'I must have been napping,' said Glitz. 'Remind me, was this a profit-making project, or –' he shuddered – 'a philanthropic one? No, don't tell me. I can guess.'

'You said you were on board with it!' Mel insisted.

'I talk in my sleep!'

Mel was never going to change him.

And she was just fine with that.

They would travel forward in stardust and hope.

And their future was going to be …

Space-tacular.

Afterword

Returning to *Doctor Who* in 2022 as Melanie Bush was both a joy and a surprise. Mel first travelled with the Doctor through 20 episodes in 1986–87, and sharp-eyed readers have likely spotted references to all six of those original stories in this novel …

The Trial of a Time Lord parts 9–12 (aka *Terror of the Vervoids*)
The Trial of a Time Lord parts 13–14 (aka *The Ultimate Foe*)
Time and the Rani
Paradise Towers
Delta and the Bannermen
Dragonfire

Outside the TARDIS, I have been fortunate to appear on stage and screen for over fifty years! I couldn't resist sneaking some of those productions and the roles I played into this book. There's a list over the page – how many did you spot?

(The bold text shows you what to look out for when you flick through the pages!)

Opportunity Knocks (contestant)
Carmel **Kazemi** in *EastEnders*
Roz in **9 to 5**: *the Musical*
Kate (and later Mabel) in **The Pirates of Penzance**
Peter Pan in *Peter Pan*
The Masked Dancer (contestant **Squirrel**)
Lena **Marelli** in *Bugsy Malone*
Rumpleteazer in **Cats**
Baby June in *Gypsy*
Violet Elizabeth Bott in **Just William**
Miss Adelaide in **Guys and Dolls**
Stephen Sondheim's **Old Friends** (performer)
Lilac Fairy in **Sleeping Beauty**
Junior Showtime (performer)
Bonnie Butler in **Gone with the Wind**
Felicity Kim **Frogmorton** in *Wombling Free*
The Saturday Starship (presenter)
Dancing on Ice (contestant)
The Lady of the Lake in **Spamalot**
Roxie Hart in **Chicago**
Sally in **Me and My Girl**
Aladdin in **Aladdin**
Betty Johnson in **Marple**
Charlie in *Charlie Girl*
Muriel in **Dirty Rotten Scoundrels**

Acknowledgements

Special thanks to Jacqueline Rayner and Steve Cole, whose brilliance and expertise have made this entire project utterly joyous and inspiring.